GIACOMO'S SEASONS

Autumn Hill Books

AB

a novel by
Mario Rigoni Stern

Giacomo's
SEASONS

translated from the Italian by
Elizabeth Harris

CONTENTS

ACKNOWLEDGEMENTS

I wish to thank the many people who read this translation and provided me with so much useful feedback: my classmates in the translation workshop at the University of Arkansas; John Behling; and my teachers, Miller Williams, John DuVal, and Louise Rozier. I also wish to thank the University of North Dakota for its support of this project. Thank you to the publisher of Autumn Hill Books, Russell Valentino, for all his careful work and insight. I wish to thank Mario Rigoni Stern's family, his wife and especially his son, Alberico, who has been so generous with his time and help over the years. Finally, I wish to thank and recognize the late Mario Rigoni Stern for his lovely book and also for his kind visit with me many years ago in Asiago, where we shared some beers and he sang me "The Song of Monte Nero" while we sat in his kitchen.

1

I went by and no one was around. The houses, silent, inside and out. In the distance you could hear a dog barking, and up in the sky two crows cawing. The snow had come low, covering Moor Hill, but even though it was cold, no smoke rose from the chimneys. All the doors were locked tight, the shutters pulled over the windows.

I remembered who used to live here, door by door: ever since I was little I'd come up here from town to play with the boy who shared my desk at school. I remembered where the cows used to be, the horses, the donkey. And the well-kept vegetable gardens, and the pump gushing icy cold water that was first white in your glass, then clear, as the bubbles rose and vanished.

The door of the oldest, smallest house wasn't quite shut. Maybe someone had gone in to have a look around, thinking he'd buy the place and renovate it as a vacation cottage. But after hearing how most of the owners were scattered through France, Australia, and the Americas, he'd given up on the idea. Or maybe it was some kids passing by who'd gone in — you never know where those kids come from or where they're going. Maybe they'd forced the door to spend the night, then left again the next morning.

The door's glass panes were missing, with pine boards hammered across instead, and there was no lock or bolt now, just a piece of wood jammed through the door handle and a strand of wire running from the handle to a nail between the stones in the wall. After knocking, calling hello, I went inside. The silence and shadows were so charged with memories, it seemed like they wanted to talk.

Cockleburs and nettles had grown up in front of the small eastern window, blocking the view of the landscape outside. All you could see was a sliver of sky.

There was still a little packed, hard ash in the black fireplace, like what you'd find at the bottom of a tomb. Magazines full of ads and naked women were scattered around on the floor, and when I pushed them aside with my foot, there were dried twigs and beech leaves below. The stone sink was still in the room, and the hooks where the copper water buckets used to hang, and the cupboards for displaying the dishes. The trench stove was gone, the one they'd found in an Austrian bunker, and so were the four chairs, the bench, and the table. There was a trap door under that table, I remembered, leading down to a cellar where they kept the potatoes, sauerkraut, lard, and cured salami. And there were the wooden stairs going up toward the ceiling, low, to hold in the heat, the rafters, black with smoke. Those stairs led to the small, dark rooms above, with their thick walls and tiny windows looking east, to the woods.

The Great War hadn't destroyed this area, hadn't leveled it like other places nearby. Strangely, everything around here was left standing, even with all the artillery fire, even though these hills had been abandoned, recaptured, and abandoned again by Italians and Austro-Hungarians. Maybe because field hospitals had been set up here? — that's what the four hundred Italian soldiers buried here in three different cemeteries seemed to suggest. These old houses had just been looted and burned: the walls were the same walls from centuries ago, and so were the enormous larch-wood rafters, only scorched a little in the flames.

Now, some thirty years later, the seven doors up here only open when city people come on vacation. And the descendants of those who built these houses with stones from our mountains and trees from our woods, who repaired the houses in 1920, who started and finished their lives here, or who left for faraway places, for work or for war, those people are gone now. The vacationers don't build fires in the fireplaces now; on weekends, they grill their sausages outdoors. The vegetable gardens have been turned into parking places. Even the pump's gone — it got in the way of the cars. Everything's different. It's all so far away, the life in this house, completely empty now and full of silence. This is where my classmate was born, where he lived until he was twenty.

They had rebuilt the town by then, with just a few shacks left standing. The new town hall, all done in pink marble, was waiting for Prince Umberto of Savoy to perform the opening ceremony. And the six new bells were waiting, too, on logs by the church doors, for the bell tower to be finished so they could be hoisted up to the belfry. When the carpenters and tinsmiths finally completed the dome, they called in Gian Scarpa to put the cross on top and the flag for testing the wind — he was the one who'd worked on skyscrapers in Chicago without getting vertigo. And the day after Gian climbed up there with everyone in town watching, they tore off the scaffolding and all its lumber.

The six bells had arrived from Verona on March 18, 1922 — from the very same foundry that cast them the first time, in 1820. They weighed a total of eleven tons (minus the clappers), and it took two big trucks to get them up here. Matío was the largest, then came Maria, Giovanna, Toni, Rita, and Modesto. They'd been blessed with these names of saints, and from the beginning, that's how they were talked about, by name, like folks from town. According to tradition they were rung like this: Matío, for fires, for warding off storms and calling town council meetings; Maria, for l'Angelus, or evening prayer; Toni was rung for the passing of men; Giovanna for the passing of women; and then these two rang together for the funerals; all six rang out for the great festivals, for weddings, and for the Conscription Festival.

They used to say that before the Great War, not far from the site of the first log church, you could still see the pits where they cast the first ancient bells. Back then, in the 14th century, the priest had preached that the more gold and silver the bells contained, the more musical they'd sound, so the day they were cast, the towns-people tossed their rings, earrings, and necklaces into the gleaming pool. And our great grandparents said the bells rang out as bright as the larks in spring. To keep the memory, the spirit, of those precious bronze bells alive, they were melted down for the larger bells cast in 1820, with representatives from town looking on. Our six bells ringing in concert grew famous throughout the Veneto, and people would come all the way up here from the plains just to listen.

On May 15, 1916, at seven in the morning, Matío rang for the last time: everyone was to leave their homes at once — the Austrians' huge 381 mm shells had begun to destroy the town. When the refugees came back in 1919, even the bell tower was gone, and a few fragments of bell were gathered up and melted down again, a last, faint reminder in the new bells.

They sat in the churchyard nearly six years, and Nino, Bruno, Mario, Bibi, Silvano, Rino, Rocco, Toni, and all the other boys playing around by the church used to hide under them. As part of their game, some of the boys would slam the bells with an iron rod to make them ring and force whoever was hiding underneath to come out.

A few days before the Patron Festival of Saint Matthew the Apostle, the bells were hoisted up the bell tower — and they really were "hoisted" — it took winches, tackle, pulleys, ropes, all provided by the Masain Brothers, and with the whole town gathered together for one big tug-of-war to get them up there. Even the school boys were invited to join in alongside their teachers. The bells had been set at the base of the tower; one by one they were tied, then raised on a very long, thick rope running off a pulley rigged up in the belfry. People formed a long line starting at the bell tower, past the Sterns' shop, up Mezzacavalli Road to Croxebech.

Slowly, with the strength of all those arms, Matío left the ground. When he was dangling in midair, all commotion and shouting suddenly stopped — there were just two men's thundering orders as their two groups pulled at the side ropes, guiding Matío's climb. Every heart was with that great bell above. He was the first, then up, up went the others.

Giacomo, Nino, and Mario were there, too, pulling with all their might, teeth clenched, hands clenched. By evening, all six bells were in place; in a few days, they'd be ringing out for our Patron Saint Matthew. Mario's father gave the three boys ten centesimi each, and they raced to Betta del Toi's and bought three juicy, green apples to restore their strength.

3

1928 was an especially hot, dry year: it had never reached over a hundred around here before, at least not that anyone recalled. The woods spared by the war were burning now, and a bitter smoke rolled in once in a while over the town. Everyone kept watching the sky and which way the wind was blowing—if a cloud would just come and cool things off. There hadn't been a mushroom in months, no wasps, no hornets, no butterflies fluttering over the vegetable plots that by now had all turned brown. At noon the beech trees along the riverbanks were as red as at the end of October; the leaves had dried up on the birch trees and maples; the sun had withered and chewed up the grass in the meadows. The insistent, hot wind and the dewless nights made for a still summer that was like, and not like, the still of winter. Even far back in the darkest, most hidden spots in the woods, in Dante Pasch's little trough for the wild animals that he'd carved into a rock, there wasn't a drop of water left. What used to be pools of rainwater for the herds were cracked patches of ground now, with hoof prints sunk in. You could barely get any milk in the bucket from the cows' dried-up udders; at night the cows bellowed at the stars, while during the day they'd wander to the shadier spots that also used to be damp and try to find anything at all green to put in their stomachs. Cattle dealers came up here from the plains and bought the animals cheap since there was nothing left to feed them. Even the birds didn't sing anymore: their chirping was more like weeping.

Water was scarce for people, too—in some areas there wasn't enough left to wash your face. They came from the Gavelles district, three hours away on foot, bringing their horses and carts to the Rendola district, to get water from the Kerla spring, which never seemed to dry up completely. People waited in line to fill every container they had. Where did that mysterious water come from?

The Monte Dubiello forest fire was spectacular: flames climbing rocky ridges, ancient larch trees going up like torches, long flames snaking up the trunks of mountain pines. The Royal Army had to be called in, and so two battalions from the Fifty-seventh Infantry came up from Vicenza. They tried circling the fire from Basazenocio and Busa del Molton, like a military maneuver, but when the flames hit the Galli Cedroni Plateaus—and the undetonated bombs from 1916—the colonel ordered his men to fall back. A few days later the fire reached Prince Eugenio Road; finally, a furious storm started in the Valle del Portule and settled just over that mountain, and first came lightning and hail, then water by the bucketful. And so the fire died out.

But meanwhile those countless red-spruce seedlings, planted to reforest the former battle sites, had dried up past hope. September's potato crop was awful: you could barely get back what you'd planted out of that dry, rocky soil—and so tiny!—if a person didn't need to put something, anything, aside for winter, it wouldn't have been worth the effort.

Men couldn't find work: the town had been completely rebuilt; the town hall was the last project, and so, until the ground froze too hard and the snow came, people went out and broke the law by collecting bomb-shells, cartridges, bullets, barbed wire, and anything else they could get their hands on to sell at the Briata plant. Those who could left the country. The dream was America, but hardly anyone could afford the trip. Some sold their land to go. The really desperate ones went to France as a first step to America, like many had done thirty years before.

And with winter came hunger. "Go to sleep," mothers told their children, "so you won't have to think about it."

The fascist mayor, the *podestà*, had signs posted on the houses at the edge of town—*Begging Strictly Prohibited Within City Limits*—but every Friday there would still be lines of poor people downtown, both young and old, stopping at the shops, knocking at the doors of the houses. They'd say a little prayer for the people from that house who'd died and ask for a handful of cornmeal, please, or a crust of bread, or a bit of hard cheese; their thanks, then, so grateful: "God bless you !"

At night, everyone went to bed very early, and even the groups gathered at the stables broke up early to save on lamp oil. The long winter of hunger had begun, and men and women would push their little carts up rocky country roads for hours on end, finally making their way into the Sterns' courtyard, asking for credit on two hundred kilograms of cornmeal for polenta.

"We'll find a way to pay you," they said.

"We have a house full of children."

And then Signor Toni told his sons or his clerks, "Give them what they need and mark it down in the ledger."

On February 11, on a freezing afternoon — after that dry, burning-hot summer came an icy cold winter! — the bells were ringing loudly and everyone wanted to know what the celebration was for. They found out the next day, when Archpriest Don Guido preached at early mass and the *podestà* posted the news: the State and Church had come to terms. Mussolini and Cardinal Gasparri had signed a treaty. At school, the teachers explained this great event.

And when Giacomo got home — starving, the two tiny potatoes and cup of milk from breakfast long since gone — after a bowl of barley minestrone with a slice of polenta, he told his mother and grandmother what he'd learned from his teacher, Elisa: "Il Duce made peace with the Pope. Now they're the two bosses in Rome. One rules souls. The other rules bodies. One rules the State. The other rules the Church."

His grandmother was listening closely. "And so ends the story of September 20, 1870, when the Septembrists from town rang our bells to celebrate the taking of Rome. And Monsignor Perbacco cursed them for it."

"What story's this?" his sister, Olga, asked. She was knitting a pair of cotton socks. "Tell me, Nonna."

"It was Mayor Silvagni's Berrette Rosse party members. They forced the bell-ringer to give them the keys because we had our civic right to ring the bells."

The next month elections were held, and Saturday, March 23, the school boys got the whole day off. On Friday afternoon, they left school, happy and noisy, and Beadle Titta Baldera just let them scream. In their notebooks, they'd been told to take down Il Duce's list of triumphs, his victory over subversives, over malaria, over blasphemy, over the devaluing of currency, and even over house flies.

The boys were to have everyone at home read the list, too, because the town was being encouraged to vote "yes" to the question: "Do you approve of the following deputies appointed by the Fascist Grand Council?"

Giacomo's grandmother and mother read the notice. "But we can't vote," his mother said, "and anyone who can—like your father—is off in France."

"But why can't women vote?" Olga asked. "Don't we count for anything at all?"

"Never mind," her grandmother told her. "Il Duce's not the one who puts minestrone in the pot."

In May, their grandmother figured out a way for them to buy a half-sack of potato seeds which they carefully planted in Corda's field. In June, Blondie the cow was taken on by Galmarara's cow-herder: at the end of the summer, once they had figured up their costs in pasture-to-milk, they'd ask for the corresponding amount in cheese.

4

In class 3A there were forty-five boys. On October 7, their teacher talked about lichen, moss, grasses, shrubs, and trees; and spores, roots, and stems; and branches and leaves; and flowers, fruits, and seeds. At the end of the lesson she asked each of them to bring in a different kind of twig the following day. A botanist would be coming to class to discuss the trees the twigs had come from.

Like always, on the way home, Giacomo joined his friends who lived nearby, and after the half-hour walk, he entered his family's small kitchen where the minestrone was on the fire. His grandmother filled a bowl for him and set it on the table by the polenta. He ate quickly.

"Your mother and Olga are out in the field digging potatoes," the old woman said. "They're waiting for you."

He got up and took the kindling hatchet from the fireplace.

"What do you want with that hatchet?"

"I have to cut a little branch for my teacher. It's today's homework."

His grandmother, muttering something, took his bowl to the sink, and after Giacomo drank a ladle of water from the bucket, he left again, shutting the door behind him.

He set out for Spilleche, for the small communal fields, plowed and terraced with their low dry-stone walls. It was a nice afternoon: the wind had swept the woods and mountains clean, but now you could see those places even better where the battles had raged twelve years before. The migrating chaffinches, fluttering into the trees to rest a while from the long journey, chirped to their companions who wanted to go on.

"Here I am, ready to help," Giacomo said when he reached his mother and sister in the field.

"Did you eat?" his mother asked. "Then sort the potatoes and put them in sacks — it gets dark early this time of year. What's the hatchet for?"

"I have to cut a little branch for my teacher."

"So she'll have something to whip you with?" Olga asked.

Giacomo stooped to gather potatoes: those damaged by the hoe they'd eat first; the most beautiful ones for sowing, then eaten after that; the smallest for the pig and the hens. When they only had a few rows left, his mother straightened up, then leaned on her hoe and told Giacomo: "Go fill the canteen at the spring. It's hot out today."

Maria del Nin was a little ways away, digging up potatoes in her field. "Giacomo," she shouted, "are you going for water? Do me a favor — my canteen's empty, too."

They were Austrian canteens, made in Bohemia of enameled metal, and found in the abandoned barracks. After ten minutes the boy had returned with cool, fresh water from the Renzola spring. Bepi dei Pûne, who'd been down in his field, leveling out the ground and burning dried stalks, now climbed up to drink some of that water and, really, to see the women's harvest. Giacomo asked him where he could find an unusual tree, a rare tree. "Our teacher told us to bring a branch to school. But they can't all be the same. What kind should I get?"

Bepi had just come back from military duty: they'd sent him far away, into the cavalry in Sicily instead of the nearby Alpini forces, like the other men from the area. That was because he'd been in the riot of June 1920, after the government officials here had wanted to end all aid for those refugees who still didn't have homes to live in or land to farm. Bepi smiled, pleased by Giacomo's question. "And who is this fine teacher?" he asked.

"The cripple," Giacomo said.

"Don't call her that," Bepi scolded. "Your teacher, Elisa Runz, was a beautiful girl. What happened to her was terrible." Then he said: "In Sicily I saw so many strange trees. Palm trees, carob trees, orange trees, flowering ash trees you could get syrup from. But none of those grow around here! And you certainly can't go all the way down *there* for a branch! Here you can get a branch from a silver birch tree, and then there's the juniper, the aspen, the pine, the ash, the maple, the linden, the rowan. But if you go behind Zai's shed you'll find a wild cherry tree, its leaves all turned red. I bet your teacher'd like that one. I think it's a beautiful little tree."

The potatoes dug up from the rocky soil were all in sacks. The women were sitting, resting on the terraced hillside, watching the town below, nestled among the mountains in their fall colors. Bepi lit his pipe. Giacomo went to find the branch Bepi had suggested. Soon he was back, holding his branch up, taking care not to damage the leaves.

The sun sank behind Pasubio, already topped in white, and the crows cawed to each other, flying high, circling together before going to roost in the trees. A blackbird pecked at the turned-up soil. Bepi tapped out his pipe and helped the women load the sacks onto their small carts, and they set out together on the Rossebech trail. By their district, they could already see smoke rising from the chimneys.

When they reached the Goazbech trail, they hurried the rest of the way. Giacomo and Olga carried in the sacks of potatoes and emptied them into the bins down in the small cellar dug out from the rock. Their mother stoked the fire, and the smoke nosed around at the top of the fireplace before creeping up the chimney.

Dusk had fallen; the small window showed only a glimmer of light: the red sky was turning purple. Giacomo went for two buckets of water at the pump and stopped in the doorway to admire his cherry branch: he'd set it in the small brass shell casing his grandmother had bought from the Polish prisoners. His mother went out to the stall to milk Blondie, going dry now since she was about ready to calve.

For dinner they had salted, boiled potatoes, a little milk, and one egg each. The lantern on the beam over the table sent their shadows looming against the wall, but the light didn't reach the kitchen corners. The fire had died down; the coals were turning to ash. Giacomo got up from the table and took a handful of small potatoes from his pocket, scraped them clean, then buried them under the coals with the fireplace shovel: in the morning they'd still be warm, and sweet-smelling. His grandmother stacked the plates and spoons in the sink; his mother took the lamp off the beam and set it in the middle of the table, then she sat down and started darning a pile of large cotton socks. Olga quickly rinsed off the dishes and saucepan. She was smoothing her hair. "I'm going to meet some friends at the Nappas' stall. I'll be back by nine."

"Remember," her mother said, "I'll be waiting for you."

Giacomo got his third-year textbook from his bag and turned to page 215, the start of the chapter on Giuseppe Mazzini and the Association of Young Italy. "'The Bandiera brothers,'" he read out loud. "'Thanks to the work of the *Carbonari*, the struggle for the unification of Italy had begun. Painful experience had taught more efficacious means for achieving final victory'—Mama, what does 'efficacious' mean?"

"I think it means 'powerful.' Keep reading."

"'... for them to win, above all else, the Italians needed to join forces in a concerted effort from the Alps to the Islands ... Mazzini was moved by the sad spectacle of the exiled *Carbonari*'—Mama, what does 'exiled' mean? Someone who leaves home? Is Papa exiled?"

"No, your father emigrated. He went abroad to work. Now go on—read. And besides, Papa mines coal. He doesn't sell it like the *carbonari*."

Giacomo had stopped reading, not quite able to remember what his teacher had said the day before, about how the *carbonari* had their own code language and how Mazzini's *Carbonari* had learned it to keep the Austrian soldiers from understanding them.

"Tell me, Nonna. If the *Carbonari* were living in the mountains with their mules and making charcoal from pine wood, how did they manage to win the war against Austria?[1] Never mind—I'm getting sleepy. Let's go to bed."

He got up from the table, put his book away in his bag, and took down the lamp by the stairs; he blew on the coals in the fireplace, touched a juniper twig to them, and lit the wick of the lamp. The small flame rose, steady, glowing; lamp in hand, Giacomo climbed the stairs, his grandmother behind him.

---

[1] Giacomo is confusing the *Carbonari* in his textbook, the members of a secret society established for the unification of Italy, for *carbonari* in general, those men who work with or sell coal and charcoal. For other historical references, see the glossary at the end of the novel. (translator's note)

Little by little, as they headed off to school the next day, the usual groups of girls and boys formed on the roads leading to town. Those from the houses farthest out had left home first, just as the sun hit the top of Monte Verena; the last of them left with the sun on the bell tower dome. Giacomo was thinking of going up to Bisachese's bird snare that afternoon to ask for a siskin finch to brighten the kitchen come winter. His friend Nino wanted to come and said Giacomo could keep the bird if they went up there together.

That morning, in the community school's first classroom to the left, a small forest was born. All the boys came in, holding their branches up high, and the teacher arranged them on her desk, each one in its place. Not that those forty-five boys brought in twigs from forty-five different trees: more than one came from a spruce, a fir, a beech, a poplar; and there were also twigs from elms, lindens, larches, maples, birches; and from rowans, with their beautiful red berries; from junipers, with their blue berries; from wild apple trees, with their small green and red apples; and from cherry trees. Two of the boys living in the center of town had even gone into Remembrance Park and clipped branches off a Northern white-cedar and a silver pine. Maybe even their teacher wouldn't be able to explain all those trees. After morning prayer and the Alpine Anthem, the visiting botanist subdivided the branches into *gymnosperm*s and *angiosperms*, and then by class, family, and genus. Each student, wide-eyed, followed the lesson. The botanist would pick up a twig and have the boy who'd brought it raise his hand. And so Giacomo never ever forgot that the cherry tree belongs to the class *dicotyledoneae*, the family *rosaceae*, and the genus *prunus*, and that there are many species of cherry trees, and his was an *avium*.

5

There it was, written out on white cardboard — *Coming soon!* And that *Coming soon!* meant the Tom Mix movie. Posters of film clips had been framed together and nailed up by the church door. The largest showed Tom on his white horse, wearing his wide-brimmed hat, gazing off to the horizon.

"I bet it'll be really good," Giacomo said to Nino and Mario. But while Nino could ask his mother for the fifty centesimi for the ticket and Mario could ask his grandfather, there really wasn't anyone *he* could ask. After children's mass in the chapel, Giacomo walked home wondering what to do with his afternoon on that boring November Sunday. The children of the district would all be at Croce Pond, and someone would have come up with something, even if it just meant playing with the cannon powder lying around Perlio's fields. It was beautiful out — San Martino summer, right on schedule.

But all that next week Giacomo couldn't get the Tom Mix movie out of his head, and he decided, finally, that to earn the fifty centesimi for the ticket, he'd go scavenging in the trenches at Ghelleraut. So as soon as he got back from school, after the usual barley minestrone and polenta, he found the small army shovel and a burlap sack. "Where do you think you're going with those?" his mother asked. "Remember, you need to chop some wood for me. And don't you have homework?"

"I'm going to Ghelleraut for a little bit."

Just eleven years before, there'd been an artillery battery at Ghelleraut. Cannon fire and gas had destroyed the huge forest; shelling had chewed up the ground. This was where Captain Waschnagg and Lieutenant Kumer had positioned six ten-caliber howitzers for a direct attack on the British trench lines on the other side of the hollow. The two officers thought the dense tree cover would keep their heavy artillery from enemy view, at least until the day of the attack—the day Emperor Karl felt would decide the war. But these six guns plus five hundred light field weapons were next to nothing compared to the thousand guns of the enemy: a solid line of British and French cannon and Italian heavy artillery; and so on the night of June 15, 1918, "Operation Radetzkey" was initiated on the Altipiano—and Captain Woschnagg shouted *"Feuer!"*—and their guns were discovered at once by the flashes of light through the trees. At first the shells fell long, or short, or to the left, making a triangle all around their position. Then the shells came thick, precise. They kept shooting back, but with every volley the tall trees were exploding all around them and their defenses were crumbling. The Hungarians and Croatians initiated their attack. A storm of bombs hit the battery, bombs of all types and all calibers—gas, shrapnel, short fuse, long fuse, 75s, 105s, 152s, 280s, even 320s. The captain and most of his men died next to the howitzers; Mayer was the only gunner left. Lieutenant Kumer and Corporal Hara carried shells from their reserves while the gunner kept firing. Then, as the lieutenant and corporal were going back for more, a 320 mm put a stop to the whole business.

Giacomo couldn't have known everything that went on that night of June 15; among the craters in the ruined ground, he started hunting for lead shot, bits of copper, metal from fuses. He'd just begun scraping with the hoe his father found on Monte Zebio when he uncovered a skull, the teeth young and white. He stared at it, not sure what to do next. Finally he dug a little deeper and covered the skull back up with dirt.

As dark set in, he started for home with two to three kilos of lead in his sack and maybe a kilo of copper. He hid it all under the corrugated metal that covered the wood pile. By Sunday, he'd sell his *recupero*, his scrap metal, to Seber—he might make even more than fifty centesimi. And he wasn't going to tell his mother about it, either, or his grandmother or sister. He started splitting wood.

The following Saturday he headed to town, sack over his shoulder. There were all kinds of scrap piles in the rack-railway yard, and shells stacked up according to caliber, and a press baling barbed wire by the ton: under the station canopies there were mounds of cartridges, copper rings, and lead shot. And there were other boys waiting by the scales to sell their *recupero*; Vu had told them to watch out: Seber would try to pay one price for everything, but they should get more for copper.

Giacomo made sixty centesimi. He counted the coins, then counted them again: two nickel-plated twenty-centesimi pieces, and two ten-centesimi pieces. On the way home, going by Malgari's, he couldn't resist buying ten centesimi worth of dried, hard chestnuts: if he sucked on them a while, then chewed them slowly enough, they'd last the whole way home.

Sunday afternoon he went to catechism with the other boys from the district, and his mother had never seen him so willing to go. "I'll probably be home late," he said. "I'm going to the movies after."

"Since when do you have money for the movies?" his mother asked.

"Since I sold some scrap metal I found at Ghelleraut the other day. Tom Mix is playing."

"You should've given me that money. Then I'd buy some wool and knit you a pair of winter socks." But she let him go, not saying another word: even her boy should be able to go to the movies once a year.

Walking to town, Giacomo was thinking that if it stayed nice out, he'd go back to Ghelleraut and find some lead and copper so his mother could get her wool. But how much would that take? And what about that scary skull? At the side door where Giordano Paris was selling children's tickets, Giacomo saw Nino and Mario, and they got in line together. Even with all the pushing the line was slow because Giordano had to count the coins by five centesimi, ten centesimi, twenty centesimi.

The movie started, and here came Tom Mix, galloping along on Tony the horse, and right with him the boys were drumming their feet on the floor boards, their hobnailed shoes stirring a whirl of dust that danced in the projector beam all the way down to the big white screen. A chorus of voices read the first subtitles, then hushed — the boys were inside that wonderful story now — and so Bepi (also known as "Garibaldi") didn't really need to shout at the top of his lungs: "Kids — keep quiet!"

Mouths wide open, eyes wide open, hands waving, feet drumming with the horses' hooves, the boys followed the adventures of Tom Mix, who got there just in time at the end to free the beautiful girl kidnapped by bandits. During the last chase scene, they jumped to their feet, screaming: "Run! Hurry! — they're getting away! Run! Run!"

And every boy was running at Tom Mix's side. When the first show ended, Giordano Paris cleared everyone out to make way for the next group. Giacomo tried to sneak under the benches, but Bepi Garibaldi caught him and dragged him out by the arm. Giacomo jerked free, though, and ducked into the crowd at the main entrance, where Raimondo was taking tickets. He slipped in with everybody pushing, among all those legs, and in the confusion managed to show Raimondo the ticket stub he'd saved, and so with no trouble at all he saw Tom Mix in *The Big Diamond Robbery* a second time.

It was pitch-black out and raining on his way home, and he could feel the snow in the air, coming down from the woods. Along the way, he ran into Bepi dei Pûne and Toni the baker who were out arguing about that last hand at Rosa's. When they noticed his silent presence — he was still caught up in the movie — they wanted to know where he was coming from so late, so far past his bedtime.

"I just saw the Tom Mix movie," he told them.

"Was it any good?" Bepi asked.

"It was great! He had a horse, Tony, that ran like the wind!"

"I just don't understand," Toni the baker said, "why they have to give a horse a Christian name."

6

The winter of 1929 was brutal. America had been hard-hit by the Depression, and we were starting to feel it here, too. Everyone was waiting, hoping the snow would melt so we could go back to planting trees for the fascist forestry militia. Supplies were getting low in the cellars. At the local tavern, Toni the baker and Aspio sat talking about how people were down to just potatoes and polenta, with bread saved for the sick and women in labor—there was only one batch of bread, ten kilos worth, for everyone north of town! Bepi dei Pûne said he wished he was a shepherd again, like when he was a boy working for the Colpi family, only now instead of wages, he'd ask the Dalla Bonas for ewe lambs and a ram to start his own flock.

More than one family ate their polenta with the whey left over in the cauldron from the milk—the dairy cooperative sold whey at ten centesimi a bottle.

And Nin Sech, Piero Perlio, and Tita Capo came back from America: they'd left here in '23, after all the rebuilding was done. Putting in ten or more hours a day in the mines, they'd managed to set aside a good amount. Piero got married, and Nin started looking around for some land to build Maria her house: he had married her right before he left, and then the day after the wedding, they'd gone up Monte Colombara to hunt for cartridges, shrapnel, and other *recupero* to trade for food.

When the three friends found out the Sterns wanted to sell off some property, they made an offer right away and got a good price. The Zai family bought one field and some woodland for their large herd of cattle; Tita Capo got Round Meadow; Nin and Tita went in together on Corda's woods (in bad shape now from all the cannon fire and trench-digging); and finally, Piero and Nin bought some nice fields and a pasture. Now it was time to get to work! So after filling in the trenches and piling up the rocks, they prepared the fields for their crops, hay, barley, and potatoes, watched all the while with envy.

When the larks were back singing on the slopes of Poltrecche and Moor Hill, Matteo got his draft notice. First he had to report to the battalion supply depot in Bassone for his uniform and gear. Then he joined his outfit in Gorizia. There were men from home with him: Bepi Pegola, Domenico Puncin, Tita Camparubar, and others. Captain Paolo Signorini—you could tell the captain really liked our boys—had them all assigned to his company. In Gorizia they met up with the other soldiers from town who'd gotten their discharge, and according to tradition, the recruits had to buy the "gray hairs" a round.

After training, the Oath to Constitution and King, target shooting (Matteo, Bepi, and Tita were designated sharpshooters, complete with the M91 rifle badge on the jacket), they set out for summer field maneuvers, on foot and wearing their packs. They passed through the Valle dell'Isonzo, reached Tolmino, Caporetto, Plezzo, then hiked all the way from Canin to Mangart—those same mountains where their older brothers had fought in the winter of 1915-16. On Monte Kukla, Captain Signorini told the story of how their battalion had attacked on February 14, 1916, but "with the high snows and enemy counterattack, things didn't go so well." On May 10, the battalion attacked again, and troops from Bassano, Ceva, and Saluzzo took the peak. But the captain didn't mention what everyone knew already—what the survivors had spoken of when they got home—the storm of Austrian bombs on that mountain, and all the Alpini troops, wounded or dead. And the death notices that started arriving, brought to our doors by the mayor and the archpriest.

Then, Captain Signorini went on, the troops in these mountains were joined by the Sette Comuni battalion, with its recruits serving as foot soldiers, its veterans as drivers; in early June, though, the battalion was transferred back to the Altipiano: on a quiet night the Austrians had shouted that they'd taken the Altipiano, and our men would have to pass by them to return home. The Alpini troops, the men from Bassano and the Sette Comuni, climbed out of the trenches; the Austrians held their fire; and the commanding officers had to hurry the men back to defend their own houses.

Matteo and the others felt a tug of emotion, being in these mountains they'd heard so much about. If our mountains, Ortigara, Zebio, and the Melettes, were familiar, these mountains, so distant and rocky and covered in snow even in summer, were mysterious, tragic.

They reached the Valle Trenta and after resting a while continued their field maneuvers. One day as they climbed up Monte Nero, the captain told them how Lieutenant Pico and the Alpini troops of the Exiles Battalion had taken the mountain. Then in memory of that battle, the captain had them sing "The Song of Monte Nero," right there, on the peak:

> On June 16 at break of day
> let the weapons fire! Oh,
> the Third Alpine is on the way
> coming to take Monte Nero!
> Yes, I lost my pals aplenty
> coming to take the mountain,
> all so young, not even twenty,
> never to see day break again....

Matteo felt himself shivering when the captain gave the order to present arms. They finished, finally, by scaling Monte Tricorno, roped together, and they reached the border — there was Austria, there was Yugoslavia, but they didn't look any different from Italy.

Back in the barracks in Gorizia, the days seemed longer, duller; toward fall, they were sent to the borders to repair some mule-tracks and footpaths. And that was better, partly because they got extra rations, too, three hectograms of bread, a quarter-liter more wine, and one lira added to the usual thirty centesimi. Near Christmas, Matteo got his first leave, seven days plus travel time. He could afford the train ticket: he'd managed to set aside seventy lire. And on Christmas morning, after early-morning mass, he could even offer Olga a cup of hot chocolate.

7

Giacomo passed fourth grade with a good report card, his best marks in math and reading. When he came home after the last day of school, his mother told him that during vacation he'd be looking after his godfather Ménego's cows. He'd get lunch and supper there and one hundred lire at the end of the summer. This would be better than working in someone else's pastures, she told him: Ménego's were close, so he could come home at night to sleep. It was a nice summer, hot, with the occasional storm. Like always.

When the cows were in the shade, chewing their cud, Giacomo would go a short distance into the woods, where he'd find strawberries, blueberries, and raspberries to eat, or else he'd look for mushrooms and carry them home at night in his cap. Keeping an eye on the cows, he'd also scoop up any lead shot or cartridges lying around, which he planned on selling when school started, to come up with the five lire needed to join the fascist youth group, the *Balilla*. Then *he'd* have a uniform and skis, too, just like his friends from town.

One day in early August, a bad storm developed off Lake Garda. Soon it rolled in over our mountains, and hail came down the size of quail eggs, and thunder and lightning shook the valleys. Giacomo saw lightning strike a nearby larch tree — it was sliced wide open, from crown to roots, as if split by an axe from the clouds. He was alone and scared, huddled in a trench; after the lightning, his mouth was filled with the strange taste of sulfur. Four terrified calves bolted, ran in circles, jumped the fence, and disappeared into the woods. Giacomo was too scared to go after them. He screamed their names at the top of his lungs, but they couldn't hear him for the storm.

When it was over, when there was clear sky to the west and the larks above were singing again, he ran to his godfather's to tell what had happened. They set out, a search party of three, looking for the calves, calling to them; finally, just before nightfall they heard Clever Girl's cowbell in Val di Nos and the others were there, close by.

Of course Giacomo was late getting home that night. His mother and grandmother had been worried—especially his grandmother, who'd remembered when Lena Nappa was just a girl, years ago, and how she'd been struck by lightning on a day like this while out grazing the cows on Barhutta's pasture. Giacomo was still soaking wet; his mother stoked the fire and had him strip down to his underwear, then she hung his clothes up to dry and his grandmother stuffed his shoes with chopped-up straw.

By the end of summer vacation, he'd collected a nice stockpile of cartridges and lead shot, and about three kilos of copper. Every night when he got home, he emptied his pockets into a munitions case (the same kind we all used to keep under the bed for storing our underclothes). His mother knew what he was doing, and she'd allow it, only he wasn't to go near any detonators or fuses—they could go off in his hands, like what happened to Bruno dell'Ebene. And that went double for lethal grenades. She was thinking she could buy some hanks of wool from Piero Ghellar with that *recupero*, and for once, she'd even let Giacomo go to the movies. Instead, one night when school was starting, she was very surprised to find out that he wanted to use his *recupero* to buy a *Balilla* membership card.

"But what good's a piece of paper with your name on it?" his grandmother wanted to know: she always paid close attention to everything going on in the house.

"All my friends in town are *Balillas*. And besides, I get a uniform, and when it snows, I get a pair of skis."

"You mean like a soldier's uniform?" his mother said. "But you're all still just babies with milk mustaches."

"They'll give me a ski outfit and a wool cap and long socks and skis and gloves."

"All that for five lire? That's a good deal," Olga said.

"I don't know why, but I don't like it," his mother said. "I guess, though, if they're giving you all those things for five lire, go ahead."

One morning Riccardo Pûn went to Seber's, hauling the *recupero* he'd found on Monte Zebio with the Zai family cart and horse, and Giacomo loaded up his stuff, too. So he had nine lire in his pocket and four more that he handed over to his mother for his fifth-year textbook, which would cost twelve lire at least.

One September day before the Saint Matthew Fair, Nin the postman came by with a money order for Giacomo's mother. It was from France, from her husband—at last! Four times a year, he'd send nearly everything he'd managed to save, keeping just enough to live on. He'd emigrated three years earlier, in '27, when there weren't any jobs left around here and Tita Sponzio had mentioned one day at the town hall that they were looking for miners in France, around Metz. The men left these hills in large numbers. Nearly all of them were ex-Alpini soldiers who'd dug tunnels and trenches during the war, so it wasn't very hard to get the classification "miner" on their passport, which, back then, was just a slip of paper, a form reading, "Passport hereby granted, valid three years, destination France." That slip of paper was folded up in their jacket pocket when they left, and they carried the familiar munitions case that they'd gotten from the weapons depot, only this time instead of 105 mm shells, the case held sweaters, socks, three shirts, one pair of corduroys, two kilos of bread, and a hunk of cheese; when they left that April morning, the cuckoo bird was singing a song that filled them with regret—*he*, at least, was coming home.

After traveling almost two days, with three train connections, they reached Metz, then learned at the *Bureau du Travail* that they weren't all going to be kept together: some of them were being sent to Orne, others to Boulay Moselle. Though hired as qualified miners, they didn't do any mining—they loaded carts and pushed them up the tracks. One man to a cart.

Italy and France had fixed salaries at fifty-five francs a day for miners and forty-four francs for unskilled tunnel laborers, but in the Lorraine Province, the mining companies came up with something different: here you were paid by every ton of coal dug out and loaded onto the trains. So a miner never actually earned the two governments' set wages — he was lucky if he got forty-two francs, working ten hours a day. For the unskilled laborers loading and pushing the carts, the pay was 2.10 francs per cart — if a load didn't add up to a ton, though, it didn't count. And the distance you had to run between places to load and unload didn't count, either; where you worked was decided by the mine foremen, who always played favorites.

Load and push. Unload and get back to the tunnel to load. Keep pushing, your sweat and spit mixed with coal dust. Once in a while, a ladle of water to rinse your mouth, to clear your throat, a handkerchief looped to your belt to wipe your forehead, your eyes. All this to earn your 31.50 francs a day; so you can pay the mining company your rent at the "block" — that set of shacks thrown together with bricks and wood, twenty guys to a shack; so you can buy your food at the mess hall, your heating coal, your lamp oil, your bottle of beer. They give with one hand and take away damn near all of it with the other, till there's hardly a thing left to send to the family.

Finally, after six months' work, Giacomo's father managed to save up enough to send home the first money order to pay off his trip and the few things he'd brought with him. Now he sent a money order every three months, and the one needed for buying their winter supplies at the Saint Matthew Fair was always on time.

"Hello!" Nini the postman called, "I've got your money order here from France." Though Nini had been out walking for three hours, they had nothing in the house to offer him. No coffee, no wine. They apologized, but he said, "It doesn't matter. It's hot out today — I'll just take a glass of cool pump water."

The next morning Giacomo's mother went to the post office, the money order tucked in her purse, and with Signora Ninella watching, she dipped the quill in the official ink and signed her full name, first her maiden name, then her married name as it appeared on the money order. Bepi della Posta counted out the money and pushed it through the cashier's window.

"Now the missus counts it," he said.

25

As she counted, she was filled with emotion, which happened every time. So much money — so confusing — a thousand thoughts at once. How to divide up the money? She had to save for the pig: eighty to a hundred and ten lire. There was the bread from Toni the baker, about fifty lire since July: a half kilo every day, eight hectograms on Sunday. Giacomo needed a new pair of shoes: his were worn out and too small besides — and he wasn't going to school with his feet wet. Maybe he could make do with a pair of clogs, but clogs didn't hold up so well. Now, what else? — Olga needed that undershirt.

She crossed the piazza and went into the church to say a prayer to Saint Giovanna for her husband. Afterwards she sat down in the last pew to think over her bills a little more. Then she left.

She went to the Sterns' shop to pay off what she bought on Sundays when she came to town for mass: her oil, sugar, pasta, rice, flour, and soap. Mosè figured up her total in the account book she'd brought along, and it matched what he had in his ledger: one hundred and three lire. She paid. Mosè, who'd been with her husband in the war, wrote "Paid in full" and signed his name, then gave her some quince jam at a discount. She'd thought her bill was going to be higher, so she also asked for two hectograms of their cheapest coffee beans to roast for when her mother was feeling poorly, plus one can of Frank chicory, one packet of Elephant dried milk for the occasional *caffellate*, one big piece of laundry soap, and one kilo of saponin. She even had enough to buy two hectograms of bologna, thinly sliced, for their noon meal on Sunday.

That night, after everyone went to bed, Giacomo's mother rose from where she'd been sewing by the fire and brought the lamp over to the table. She found a quill and notebook in her son's satchel, and she opened the notebook, undid the stitches, and removed a sheet of lined paper. Then she found a small bottle of ink and started to write: "Setember 8 1930. Dear Huzband, I hope this finds you in good health like us. Yesterday I recieved your Money Order for seven hundred francs and today I went to the Post Office to cash it. I paid Toni the baker three months bread, I also paid the Sterns, Signor Mosè sends his regards. At the Santmathew fair we will buy a nice *mascetto*. I am also thinking of having Tan Millar make Giacomo a pare of shoes he really needs them since he grew. And I will also buy fifty kilograms of zala flour for winter. After Santmathew we will harvest our potatos from Corda's field. I think its a better crop than last year. So add some lintels and we will have that soup you love so much. We all expect you for Christmas make sure you come. Please dear Huzband always be careful in the mine. I think of you all the time. Yours truly, your fatheful wife." She signed her married name and first name; she folded the letter and slipped it under the small brass shell casing on the shelf; in the next few days—maybe even tomorrow morning—she'd go to town to buy an envelope and get his address off the money order receipt.

Those days of fall, Giacomo and the other boys from the area went up to the Taltebene forest for firewood. They used pruning hooks to scrape clean the tree trunks and dried branches that were scattered under the brush, and then they piled the wood onto makeshift sleds and dragged it to the mule-tracks from the war, which they could reach with their wheelbarrows. The boys' teacher, Andrea, loved going for firewood, too, on those quiet afternoons. His favorite was beechwood with its twisted trunks, its roots winding around the rocks underground. He'd use his pick to turn up the rocks, his hatchet for chopping the exposed roots, and then he'd crank at the tree trunk with his mallet until he tore it from the ground like an ogre's tooth. If the boys ran into him, they'd lend a hand rolling the tree stumps down through the woods, past the artillery sites and trenches that told of a time when the mountain had belonged first to one side, and then the other.

8

Olga was a beautiful girl now. At night, in their gatherings, the young men liked her close by. Olga, Maria, Tonina, Bianca, and Nina made for a lively group—the five of them together even felt brave enough to poke fun at the boys, who were sometimes intimidated by all the teasing. Except Riccardo: not yet twenty, he still knew exactly what to say to make the girls blush. Matteo had completed his military service, and even last Christmas on leave, his interest in Olga was obvious. Now on Sundays he could hardly wait to walk her to mass, along the road to town. In late fall, according to ancient custom, Matteo gathered his "civic quota" of beechwood, and then he went to help Olga and Giacomo, who'd been assigned to collect theirs in a remote spot above the mule-track.

One November evening before supper, he got up the nerve to knock on her door. He'd been trying to think of some reason to come by and finally settled on asking Giacomo to catch two male titmice for him to keep as song birds. It was already getting dark in their small kitchen, so the red rising on Olga's face didn't show in the lamplight. Giacomo's mother, understanding at once that the titmice were just an excuse, broke the embarrassed silence: "But what do you want with two titmice?"

"Well, their singing's nice," he said, "and they make everything cheerful. They're good company."

"That's right," Giacomo's grandmother said. "Titmice are cheerful. Now sit down and have a potato. Here's salt to dip it in." Olga had told her about Matteo. So she'd do her part. After all, Matteo was a good man, and handsome besides.

"No thank you," Matteo said. "Maybe I'll come by some other time." But he took a potato from the bowl and gnawed it where he stood.

And he did come by, with one excuse after another—even

Giacomo knew Matteo was there for his sister. Finally one night he declared his love for Olga and asked if he could stay.

"It's all right with me," her mother said. "Come when you like. Make it after supper. But on one condition"—she pointed to the alarm clock on the shelf—"at nine thirty you go home, and we go to bed. And, of course, you'll need to speak to her father. He might be back for Christmas."

That night Matteo even stayed for supper: boiled potatoes, mashed with a stick in the bronze pot, hot bacon grease and sage poured on top. After dinner Giacomo set three logs on the embers and blew through a rifle barrel till they caught fire. The adults dragged chairs over; Giacomo sat on the hearth. Matteo rolled a cigarette of fine-cut tobacco.

"So how's work?" Giacomo's mother asked.

"Getting harder all the time. All you can find these days is planting spring seedlings. Or else there's searching for *recupero*—but you have to be careful—Sergeant Caregnato and Officer Rizzo are getting stricter, and they'll slap you with a fine." Then Matteo said, "I've been offered a job. Tiftellele's blasting field. It's sixteen lire a day—"

"Don't take it!" Giacomo's grandmother cut in. "That's just awful work!"

"And your husband? How's mining in France?"

"The pay would be all right if the cost of living weren't so high. And mining's not like the work around here. The risks he has to take, the coal dust...." She turned to Giacomo. "Don't you have any homework? You've been out in the woods all day!"

"Let me have a puff off that," Giacomo's grandmother said to Matteo. "Let's see if it tastes like what my poor man used to smoke."

"I have to study history for Tuesday," Giacomo said. "I'll get my book." His satchel was by the stairs; he found his schoolbook and went back to the hearth. He read in the firelight, first to himself, then out loud: "'The Italian intervention. The people decided the hour had come to tear the Austrian yoke off our unredeemed lands, and so, with unbridled enthusiasm, they asked that war be declared on Austria—'"

"We didn't ask a thing," Giacomo's grandmother said. "Poor Tönle got it right."

"'Benito Mussolini, great man of humble birth, today Il Duce of Fascist Italy, set the people's spirit on fire with his passionate speeches and patriotic writing.'"

"Nonsense," Giacomo's grandmother said. "Go on. Look up when we were refugees in '16 and then when we came back home."

Giacomo flipped ahead, skimming the pages, murmuring as he went, and then: "Found it. 'In the Valle dell'Isonzo, the Alpini troops, our fine mountain boys, overran the Austrians' impregnable position at the top of Monte Nero. The Austrians sought revenge: in May 1916, after a horrific bombardment that destroyed our defenses, they overwhelmed our lines at Trentino with their huge army and vast cannon fire. It took a month of steady battle, but our men recaptured nearly the entire area they had been forced to surrender as a result of the surprise attack....'"

On one page, there was even a photo with the caption, "Foxhole in the Mountains": the photo showed some soldiers in helmets and a proud officer with a mustache, posing by a foxhole among the trees.

"Looks fake," Giacomo's grandmother said. "This picture was taken in our own woods — I think I know where. Keep reading."

"'And so we must salute Benito Mussolini, one of the deciding factors in our war and our triumph, and moreover, savior to Italy in that terrible period following the war.'"

She didn't say anything now. Maybe she was thinking about her husband, killed on Monte Kukla; and how they'd all had to flee, leaving everything behind; and about the Spanish flu; and when they came back to their land; and then her son-in-law emigrating to France even though they'd won the war; and what sort of history was being taught in school these days instead. They all grew quiet; Matteo held Olga's hand. The coals were turning to cinders. Giacomo's eyes were nearly closed.

"We'd better go to bed," Mother decided. "Tomorrow morning early, Zai's coming to plow our field on Poltrecche."

Olga walked Matteo outside, and her mother had to shout to get her back in.

9

Those first days of December the snow came, but then it melted for the Festival of the Immaculate Conception, with a warm *bonaccia* wind from the south. Then Santa Lucia brought back the cold. On the ninth day of Christmas, the boys and girls of the district gathered round the Oba Pool Cross after supper and sang the *Stella*. Sometimes the girls would try and sing too high, the boys too low, but when they all just sang in their natural voices, the song was sweet. Sometimes they stopped singing altogether, so they could hear the carolers from the other areas. In the Bald district, they were even singing in ancient Cimbro!

Giacomo liked keeping Irene company. One still night, the moon's bright halo suggested snow, and then it started, the big snowflakes floating down onto their heads. The carolers seemed so far, far away.

The afternoon three days before the twenty-fifth, Giacomo stopped by Irene's and they went to Kunsweldele to chop down a tree. At school they'd been told that people should have a manger for Christmas, that trees were a foreign custom. But around here we'd always had trees. For one thing, they cost less: a little cotton wool for snow, some colored silk thread, some pine cones dyed crimson, a shooting star carved out of wood with a pocket knife, then painted bright yellow, and four small candles, and you had yourself a splendid, shining tree. Around sunset Giacomo and Irene cut down a small tree, deep in the woods. They skipped along through the cold snow going home, and when they reached their district, the lamps were already lit.

On the twenty-third, Giacomo's father came home. He made his way all alone that night from the station, the snow crunching under the studs of his shoes. He'd been gone three years. It seemed like thirty. From the train window, he'd watched the growing shadow of the mountains against the starry sky and the lights of the towns and cities below, growing smaller. And he finally stopped thinking about the dark mine and depressing shack that had stayed with him all the way to the border. He was nervous, almost afraid to get there.

When Giovanni reached the station he'd left from three years before, no one was there to greet him. The morning the men left had been dark as well, and Giacomo, Olga, and his wife had stood beneath the wooden awning, with all the other women and children. The men waved their hats goodbye out the train windows.

He stepped onto the platform. Tuncali the night watchman, present for all scheduled arrivals, recognized him and greeted him with restrained affection, for decorum's sake. Cecilia the postal worker saw him, too, and said hello; she was there as usual to get the mail — maybe Giovanni's letter was even in that sack, the one that said he'd be there for Christmas though he wasn't exactly sure what day.

Others got off the train, too, all of them, strangers, on Christmas vacation, with their suitcases and skis. Rucksack over one shoulder, munitions case in hand, Giovanni set out along Via Trento and Via Trieste; in the piazza in front of the town hall, two frozen fountains glowed with colored lights, spots of green, yellow, blue, and red sparkling through icy stalactites. Between the fountains, a large group stood singing in a circle. He didn't stop there, or even at the Modesto del Nazionale, for a glass of mulled wine. It was time to get home. The light ended with the school and the road turned to two gravel tracks. He could see his way, in the quiet of the night, by the stars shining on the snow. He heard carolers. The distant hills and river banks were sprinkled with houses, light trickling out the kitchens.

He was sweating from carrying his rucksack and case; the snow crackled under his mining shoes, and he remembered all the times he'd been on this road: when he was little; when his wife was just a girl, walking with her; when he got his discharge back in 1919, walking with old Tana who kept insisting, so happy, that even if everything here had been destroyed, this was still the only place on earth he'd want to be. He walked and remembered. His feet seemed to know every bump, every curve, on their own. Before the final hill he stopped and sat down to rest on one of the rock slabs lining the road; he set his munitions case next to him in the snow. And then he started laughing—this was the same rock they used to joke about, where Toni Moro saw the talking cat. The way they told it, one night on his way back from tomcatting, Toni Moro dropped his pants behind the rock wall on the other side of the road, then just as he was pulling them back up, he saw a big black cat sitting right here, watching him, so he made a snowball and threw it as hard as he could, but he missed. The cat didn't budge. It just stared at him with its fiery eyes and said, "Why don't you try one underhand!"

When Giovanni walked into the kitchen, no one said a word. "I'm home," he told them, and they all jumped up, everyone squeezing and touching him, hugging and kissing him.

"Let him breathe!" Giacomo's grandmother said. "Grab his bag! Set it down!"

He looked around, taking in everything he'd left: it was all the same. Except for the Christmas tree, there in the corner, between the fireplace and window. "How beautiful!" he said.

He was the one who insisted on rekindling the fire, his every move familiar to him. Then he wanted to know what there was to eat—all the excitement of seeing him again had made them forget to even ask if he was hungry!

"There's polenta," Giacomo's mother said, "and some of Blondie's milk. And fresh liver sausages, too. We killed the pig last week." She looked at Giacomo. "Go cut down three." He took a knife and raced up the stairs to the room over the kitchen, where their meat was hanging from the rafters — salami, *musetti*, bacon, and liver sausages made from liver, lard, organs, and red meat flavored with cloves, pepper, salt, and a splash of grappa.

Giacomo's father spread the coals himself with the fireplace shovel—as if he'd only been gone the day, out working in the woods, instead of away mining three years in France; he set the skillet with the three liver sausages on the small grate, and the four slices of polenta on the bigger grate below. He didn't want to eat at the table. He sat by the fire dipping polenta in the grease and now and then taking a mouthful of sausage.

"Boy, that's good," he finally said. "Is Angelo Gaiga still making our salami?" And then: "I'm so tired—I've been traveling almost two days. But I brought back some things for you." He pulled himself away from the warm fire. He set his bags on to the table and started rummaging through his things. "This is for Nonna." He held up a black wool shawl. "And this is for you." It was a flowered shawl for his wife. "Here's some stockings for Olga and three chocolate bars for Giacomo. And a nice loaf of white French bread—they call it a 'baguette.' "

"Now it's *really* Christmas!" Giacomo said. "Thank you, Father!"

"Time for bed," Giacomo's grandmother decided. "And you"—she turned to Olga—"you sleep upstairs with Giacomo and me. Leave the warmest room over the kitchen for these two. All right, take the lantern. Up we go."

10

Giacomo's father brought almost three thousand lire back from France. A small fortune! He spent that winter enjoying the quiet of his house. The first long break of his life. Sometimes in the afternoons, he played cards at Forts' Tavern with Vittorio, Ernesto, and Toni the baker. On Sunday afternoons, Toni Moro and Angelina would come up from town along with Ménego Stern, Piero, Nane Scajari, and others. Moro Ballot would arrive with some local girls; then while Vittorio strapped on his accordion, Menego Vuz would tune his guitar, and away they all went, dancing the waltz and the mazurka. A little wine and it was like carnival-time. Matteo even danced with Olga.

Matteo got a letter from Australia, from his father's brother, who'd emigrated in 1903. Uncle Nicola had married a British woman but didn't have any children. If Matteo couldn't find work, Nicola wrote, he had a job for him. Nicola had his own construction business in Melbourne; he'd started out as a bricklayer and built up the business on his own, and his nephew could be his right-hand man. Through Lloyds of Triestino, he'd supply the money for the trip right away.

Before giving his answer, Matteo wanted to think it over a few days; and he wanted to know what Olga thought, too. Finally he wrote back that he wouldn't mind going to Australia, but he was engaged now to Giovanni's daughter. His uncle came up with two solutions: "I'll pay for her trip, too," he wrote, "or else you come down here by yourself, and when you've earned enough, you send for her."

Several nights later, they talked it over for some time with Olga's family. Giacomo listened, not saying a word: he didn't like the idea of his sister so far away—he'd seen Australia on the map—it was on the other side of the world!

"It wouldn't be fair for your uncle Nicola to have to pay Olga's way, too," her father said after Matteo explained the situation. "But it wouldn't be fair for us to have to bleed ourselves dry to pay for her, either. Plus, there's her dowry to think about—"

"As far as the dowry," her mother cut in, "that's almost taken care of. Every time you sent me money from France I went by Piero Ghellar's and bought something else. All that's missing now are some sheets and blankets."

Olga stared at her, astonished. "I didn't even know!"

"You didn't *need* to know."

"But that's not the main problem," Matteo said. "Of course I'm happy about the dowry, too," he added, "but the question is—should we get married first, and then I leave, and you join me later? Or do you wait till I send you the money for the trip, and then we get married in Australia? Or even—do we get married by proxy?"

"If I might get a word in," Giacomo's grandmother said at this point. "I'd think about selling the Moor meadow for Olga's ticket."

"And then what do we give the cow for food?" Giacomo's mother said. "With that meadow, at least we've got milk on the table."

His father was quiet, thinking, watching the wood burn on the fire. Then he said, "How about this: you leave for Australia. When you've raised the money, you marry Olga by proxy, and then she joins you there."

"But who knows how long I'd have to wait," Olga said.

"If you trust me," Matteo told her, "it could work."

"So why don't we get married first?"

"And what happens if you get pregnant?" her grandmother said. "You'd make the trip with the baby? Going to Australia's not exactly a stroll to the vegetable patch!"

"Weighing the pros and cons," her father said, "maybe it would be better if your uncle Nicola paid for the trip after all. Working for him down there, you could pay him back and be done with it."

So everything was settled. Olga's father didn't waste any

time — a few days later he was at the Cariscs' sawmill buying wood to make the steamer trunks for the dowry; the wood he chose was beautiful: red spruce, and not one knothole. He and Matteo brought the wood over to Bepi Pegola's and they built two solid trunks with iron supports hammered out by Patao; then the dowry goods were carefully packed away inside, complete with three blankets and six sets of sheets.

Now that he'd decided, Matteo sent a letter off to Australia right away. His uncle Nicola answered that he'd already arranged with Lloyds of Triestino for Matteo and his bride's fare; but these letters back and forth took over three months. Everything confirmed, they got the paperwork together for their passports and the other certificates required by the Australian Consulate in Venice. Meanwhile their wedding announcement was posted on the church door and at the town hall. The wedding day was arranged so the newlyweds would be able to make the train to Vicenza after the ceremony and then catch another to Trieste, where the Oceania would be waiting to take them on their long, long honeymoon. The trunks were sent on ahead by train.

That morning, before everyone from the northern hills walked to town together, they stopped at Olga's and Matteo's for sweets, dry and dessert wines, hot cocoa, *soppressa* and other salami, new and aged cheese, rye and wheat bread, espresso and grappa. People sang and toasted the couple. The gifts were displayed on side-tables, some of them gag gifts, others more practical. Someone with the long trip ahead in mind had given the couple a deck of cards.

When the bells started their joyous ringing, everyone set out, the bride and groom in front with the wedding attendants, the two families and all the friends following behind. Giacomo told Irene, "Now we're in-laws," and took her hand.

The small procession moved on in silence: the joyful bells, the summer morning, the smell of scattered hay drying in the fields — everything in sight stirred up strong feelings. The two who were going so far away felt they were leaving these mountains, this horizon, forever. Those staying behind felt part of them was going away, too. Everyone kept walking, their hearts full.

11

From what Giacomo read in his school book, Il Duce had made our air force the strongest, the mightiest air force in the world! We had "three squadrons of fighter planes, three squadrons of reconnaissance planes, and two each of bombers and sea planes." When Giacomo pictured those squadrons, they were like the flocks — like the squadrons — of thrushes filling the bird snares in late fall. So was it all those planes of ours that made them start building an airfield on the widest, most fertile meadow in the valley? People would swap stories about how, in 1915, there used to be airplanes in the meadows around the Sbanz district — and how it was right from there that the prophet-poet Gabriele d'Annunzio took off for Trent, to drop a tri-colored flag from the sky. And then there'd been the gliders, dragged up Monte Sisemol by mule and launched off elastic cords. They'd even brought gliders from Germany. But now — to build a real airport!

They started off by taking all the Scirans' land in the Ebene district, and then the Michelonis' fields, the Zurlis', and more fields yet — from the house where the engineer lodged his *recupero* crew down almost to the Pach district: a million square meters. Cristiano Catelar took on all the contracting.

They knocked down the houses in the Micheloni district, the engineer's farmhouse, the dairy cooperative; then they started leveling out the ground, reducing the slope, bringing in over a thousand cubic meters of dirt and gravel on Decauville railcarts. So the unemployed got a little relief, though with the lira devalued by Il Duce, a worker's wages had gone down significantly in actual buying power. To get a few days' work, men even came in from the surrounding towns; they'd wait alongside the field for someone doing a poor job shoveling to be sent away, then step in and take his place.

Shovels and picks brought up remnants from the war, and every man had his sack ready—what he found made for his combined salary. Live bombs, though, at least the biggest, were set aside, to be detonated later in Petareitele's tunnel.

Children going to school and anyone wanting to get to town from the northern hills had to go farther around, now that the roads had been moved. Many, defying the guards, still crossed over the airfield under construction—a centuries-old habit is hard to break. But everyone walking in that empty space felt uneasy, cut off from something.

Many of the older people from town and the surrounding area would go spend the day watching all the frenzied work out there, and they'd shake their heads and agree how so much turned-over soil would have made such a beautiful potato field, big enough to feed thousands for a year—or what a beautiful Alpine summer pasture—enough for a hundred and fifty dairy cows. The workers had Sundays off, and the local boys, Giacomo and his friends from town, would set back on the tracks the carts pushed over at the end of the Saturday shift; they'd climb in and fly down the steep slope. And climb out and push the carts back up to fly down again; until they were tired, finally, and pushed the carts back over the way they'd found them.

Giacomo's father, Giovanni, had been hired on as a laborer, too, at 1.10 lire an hour, but after the first fortnight, he quit—he'd learned the Committee For Honoring Our War Dead was paying a good two lire for brass 105 shell casings that were then filled with flowers and set on the Italian soldiers' graves in the military cemetery. He knew of some Austrian batteries not too far away, and he also remembered a tunnel where a lot of shell casings had been hidden after the bombings, maybe with the plan of using them over. That was in 1920 when he found the tunnel, the same year Giacomo was born; he'd collapsed the entrance because back then he'd had better things to keep him busy, but now....

He started looking and found the tunnel again. But as he cleared the entrance, he realized someone else had beaten him to it—the tunnel was empty. What a disappointment! All the more so when he suddenly remembered how one night, back in his shack at the French mine, he'd told Nane Runz about this secret tunnel, and then the following Saturday, Nane Runz had collected his wages from the bookkeeper and caught the next train home to Italy. He'd even heard it from the Forts some time later that Nane had sold a cartload of casings to Seber.

He switched to looking in the Gastagh district, where there were some Austro-Hungarian military cemeteries; this was also where old man Tana had blown up the big cannon. Patiently, methodically, making use of what he'd learned in the war, he did manage to dig up some 152 shell casings, but they were too big for the graves, so he had to settle for selling them to Seber at twenty centesimi per kilo.

When Giacomo came home from school, after eating, he'd hike up to where his father had arranged to meet him on the mountain and help carry the *recupero* back down.

But this luck didn't last: others had heard what the Committee For Honoring Our War Dead wanted, and in little over a month, on every soldier's grave there was a shell casing filled with wild flowers that the women and children had brought. When Il Duce declared war on Ethiopia, though, all the casings were taken away again, sent off to the munitions factories to be recycled.

12

How could anyone stay inside on a beautiful spring afternoon and just do homework when the cuckoos were singing in the woods and the larks were singing in the sky over the meadows? So after school, before Nino and Mario took Via Monte Ortigara and Giacomo headed up the hills toward home, the boys decided they'd eat, then go to the Ghelleraut woods and hunt for morels, nests, and cartridges. They'd meet up at Bersaglio.

And they all got there right on schedule, and started off. Behind the low stone wall along the road to the Villa Rossi, Mario found a stonechat's nest, with six tiny, sky-blue, brown-speckled eggs inside; he'd spotted the nest when the female bird flew away.

"Don't touch the eggs!" Giacomo said. "If they were just laid, the mother might abandon them."

Also behind this wall, Nino noticed the tips of five bullets poking through some moss. He pulled the moss aside and found four Austrian cartridge clips.

"Right behind here's where a soldier hid," Giacomo spoke up again, "so he could shoot at our men. These clips must've fallen from his cartridge belt." That was Giacomo for you: find something, and there had to be a fact, a why, an answer. Like when they first heard the buzzing, then found three bumble-bee nests. "Watch out for the gray kind with the red ass. Those are really mean. But there shouldn't be too many right now. August is the best time for catching those."

Mario and Nino already knew this: every year, after the hay was cut, they hunted for bumble-bee nests along these stone slabs dividing the fields; they found the nests by stomping around to get the bees buzzing, and then they'd mark the spot with a small post. At night, they'd come back with a flask of water and a handkerchief. They'd sprinkle water on the nest and all around it, and this kept the bumble bees quiet since they thought it was raining; then the boys would drape the handkerchief over the nest and scoop up the whole thing. If you held the bundle to your ear, you could tell by the level of buzzing how many bees you'd caught. At home, the entire nest would go in a cardboard box that was set on a window sill; you'd wait two days, then poke holes in the box for the insects to get through. Sometimes they left and didn't return; other times they'd come and go like honey bees. In the fall, then, you could suck honey out from the little cells with a straw.

That day, the three boys kept hunting around, peeking under the junipers and red-spruce seedlings by the trenches. They walked along in silence, eyes to the ground, looking for morels, until they found themselves far off the trails, at the edge of a clearing.

"Hey, *Balilla* boys!" someone called to them. "Where you headed?"

Four men were sitting in the grass, obviously celebrating something: a blanket was spread out before them with glasses, a flask, some bread, salami, and cheese. Giacomo saw his father and right away recognized Nin, Angelo, and Massimo.

"Come here," his father said. "Where are you all off to?"

"We're hunting for morels."

"Any luck?" Angelo asked. "You could try the Busettes, but it's still a little early."

"Hey," Nin Sech said to Mario, "weren't you around here last year, too?"

"I always come here for morels. It's a good place. You gave me some bread and cheese."

"Sure, that was May 1, too," Angelo Castelar said. "Come sit with us — have something to eat."

They offered the boys some bread and salami; they also wanted them to have a sip of red wine; Massimo Ciorgolo asked if they had any homework.

"Yeah," Nino answered, "but today's so nice, we decided to come here instead."

"Good for you," Giacomo's father said. "We're taking the day off ourselves. Such a fine day."

The boys finished their bread and salami, thanked the men, and went back to hunting morels. When they were a little ways off, Mario asked Giacomo, "So what was your father celebrating with his friends?"

"I'll tell you," Giacomo said, "but you have to swear not to say anything. Today's May 1—May Day—the workers' festival. When they were in France, they always celebrated May Day, but it's banned here in Italy. I don't know why, but it is."

13

School let out, and Giacomo, after his final exam, passed fifth grade with a report card where the "excellents" outnumbered the "satisfactories." So, like most of the other children, he was all done with school now. At the end of each school year there were at least twenty fifth-grade classes in the district, but when it came time for registration in secondary school, there'd be only one class of girls left and one of boys. The old arts-and-trade school had been closed down by the authorities — anyone taken on as an apprentice to a craftsman, blacksmith, carpenter, or tailor counted himself lucky to be learning a trade; without pay, of course, or insurance, and the master didn't always give you a tip for the Saturday matinee, either. Some boys who'd grown up in the shadow of the church decided on going to seminary. People would ask them, half-joking, half-serious:

"So what do you want to be? A priest, a monk, or out with the cows?"

Giacomo, now free from school, felt a little wistful for the friends he'd left behind: the boys living in town and those farthest away, to the south. He wanted his mother to enroll him in school, but the registration fee and all the books just cost too much; besides, with Olga off in Australia, he was needed at home to chop wood, to work in the fields and hoe the potatoes.

On the final day of school, his teacher had asked him to read the last page of their textbook out loud: "Italy is not only beautiful but great. She has the most beautiful palaces, the most majestic, celebrated churches, which pilgrims the world over come to visit. She is admired by all for her great collections of beautiful statues and paintings, for the many signs of her glorious past; her many towers, palaces, aqueducts, and ruins of ancient towns and cities recall a time when Italy dominated the entire known world. Fascism is working, for Italy grows ever greater." This is what he'd read in his typically loud voice, but after getting his report card and singing the patriotic songs, he started thinking (in church during mass for San Luigi) that he'd never actually seen any of the things he'd read about. Still, if they were in the books, they must be true.

His friends Nino and Mario had promised that the first day of vacation they'd all go together to the small, almost hidden quarry and find some of that pink marble with the red, yellow, bright orange, and violet streaks. They were looking for some smaller chunks to make the four marbles needed to play *alt messen*—Cimbro for "throw, stop, and measure." That quarry, near Hano and behind the Monks' House, seemed pretty old—everyone knew that's where you went for the *steiner* for the game balls. And then you'd take your old files and worn-out axes to Menno's and have them forged into bush-hammers and picks for working the marble. When it came to the tools for wood and stone, Menno was the best blacksmith around. Using a spindle and bow, he'd finish the marbles, making them gorgeous and perfectly round by spinning them one by one inside a cupel carved into a cobblestone or millstone: all the color variations showed up when you licked the marbles, and you could get up to two lire for a four-piece set.

That afternoon the boys went to the Grebele marble quarry. Mario had brought along some bread and quince jam, Nino some bread and salami, and they went as far as Cola Scoa's pen before they stopped and had their snack, splitting it three ways. Too bad the wild cherries weren't ripe yet on the tree.

They chose each piece of marble with care; first they'd spit on it, wipe it on their pant leg to get a better idea of how solid the stone was and how nicely streaked, then tuck the piece in their pocket. Going down by way of the Duncheltellele trail, the boys met Matío Perlio and his son Toni (their classmate), who were bringing the sheep up to their pen behind Bersagliere Meadow.

"So what're you boys doing around here?" Matío asked.

Giacomo spoke for all three of them. "We've been looking for colored *steiner*. For *alt messen* balls."

"Good, good. And did you find some nice pieces? The marble has to be really solid, you know. Otherwise, you throw the balls too hard, they break."

Now Nino spoke up: "We know."

"*Billarkindar*," Matìo said, referring to them in the old dialect, "do you know the story of that split rock you're sitting on? When I was a boy"—and so he began—"this trench over here's where Cola Scoa had his barley field. One morning—by now the barley was full-grown—Cola came out and found his field all trampled, and most of the barley ears eaten. When he saw the bear tracks, he flew into a rage. So that very night he came back with a shotgun and hid inside this big crack in the rock. He waited and waited, almost all night, and finally, toward dawn, he heard the thrushes singing. And then he heard the bear coming down the path. He cocked his gun. The bear went out in the field to have himself a snack, and Cola fired the first barrel—but the gun misfired. Now the bear was sniffing around. It was lumbering toward him!—he fired his second barrel—lucky for him, this time the powder lit. The bear rolled over in the dirt. Cola gripped his knife and jumped out from the split rock. But the bear wasn't dead—it chomped down on his arm. Cola screamed so loud he startled the bear—it let go—and Cola plunged his knife into the bear's heart. So the bear died. I saw it lying there, dead—I was your age. They say it was the last bear in these mountains. I've never seen another."

And that was Matìo Perlio's story. The three boys, wide-eyed, got up to have a closer look at Split Rock. Here, Cola had waited, hidden from that giant bear, and that was where the barley field must have been; Toni wasn't much interested, though—God knows how many times he'd had to sit through his father's story. Mario crawled into the crack of the rock with a small branch and stretched out, aiming it like Cola Scoa's gun. "Click," he said. "Boom!" They all laughed.

Going back they stopped to fill a rusty mess kit with cannon powder; there was more powder in the fields than rocks. They were thinking about blowing up some empty Sidol jars that evening—to scare the girls.

14

After the hay harvest, every morning good and early, Giacomo and his father would climb up Camin's trail. They weren't the only ones — the last way you could earn even a little these days was by digging up *recupero* left over from the war. The three thousand lire brought home from France were going fast: there'd been Olga's wedding, and the cow they'd had to buy after being forced to sell Blondie to Titta Beccaro — "due to old age" — was what the dealer said. Their postal account book showed just three hundred lire left, to be saved for emergencies.

They walked along in silence with all the other *recuperanti* going for scrap metal. They had shovels and picks over their shoulders, burlap sacks, a little food, and those who could manage it, a bottle of milk. They'd find water dripping in some tunnel or trickling off the rocks into a trough someone had scratched out long ago.

In those places where the fighting had been nonstop and especially hard, the woods were completely gone now and the ground ripped apart, first from the trenches, then from the cannon fire. In some spots, like on Monte Ortigara, the rock had been reduced to gravel. All you had to do was scrape away the soil there to find iron, cast-iron, lead, copper, brass. And bodies.

There wasn't much profit in collecting iron — fifteen centesimi per kilo — and hauling fifty to seventy kilos some distance on your back so you could earn your seven to ten lire just wasn't worth the effort. Cast-iron paid a little more, but not much. When you'd found enough cast-iron and iron, though, you could pile it up near a mule-path and carry it down on a sled or small cart, which was a lot easier. And no one else would consider taking it, either — the same thing for wood — what you collected and piled up in plain view was sacred: anyone stealing something like that would be shunned forever by the entire community.

Lead brought twenty centesimi per kilo; brass eighty; and copper one lira and fifty centesimi. The TNT from the bombs was sold in secret to mine owners, almost always in trade for flour or wine or grappa. The *recuperanti* who'd been in the war were experts now as to the different kinds of bombs and what caliber; if the bomb was gas or shrapnel; if it was Italian, Austrian, French, British. Those who'd fought right here, in our home mountains, remembered the artillery sites quite well, and what they'd fired on. They remembered the warehouses, depots, and out-of-the-way spots where there were still things left from the war. And certain units who'd lightened their load when they had to relocate, hiding their ammunition in the crack of some rock, or in a ravine.

From the remains of the bodies, from someone's dog tags that you could still read, from knives, cans, mess kits, pipes, tobacco tins, coin purses, bottles, and medals with their special saints or madonnas, you could tell a man's battalion, his region of Italy, or where he came from in the Hapsburg Empire.

On Monte Colombara, by the Austrian trenches, there were bits of bicycle and bone. The *recuperanti* threw up their hands: "Look at that! Poor bastards! Italian infantry—hauling bicycles way up here—when you can barely keep on your feet! Where were they trying to get to? To Trent? On bicycles, through these mountains? Their commanding officers had to be crazy!"

And at the trenches on Zebio, where the Austrians had two lines of barbed wire, machine guns in a cave, outposts, and reinforced concrete pillboxes, they found human remains and Italian rifle cartridges. "How on earth," they wondered, "did these Sardinians make it this far?"

They'd take their break together, lighting a fire to toast polenta, eating what they'd brought from home, talking over what they'd found; those who'd been in the war commented on how deep the Austrian trenches were, and that they had better defenses strategically placed on more lines—at their home-base, you still couldn't get through the tangled barbed wire. They swapped stories about patrols and battles. They remembered the names of officers, both good and bad, and absurd amounts of provisions, and times when there were none. Hunting for *recupero*, they saw their war again, not from the bottom of a trench, or from a dark dug-out in the rocks, or as they'd lived it in the fits and starts of combat or shelling, but out in the open now, from above, on their feet—and the view was entirely different—more vast, more complex, more dramatic even: the bones they discovered around Agnelizza Pond were the bones of their buddies and neighbors from the Bassano and Setti Comuni Battalions; the bones they found under the pine trees on the Ponaris Mountains were the bones of the men from Brescia, in the Vestone Battalion, who'd been their flank in the trenches on Luzzo.

And they saw what their enemies saw: inside the trenches where they'd been fired on; the supply lines where the cannons had been that they never did manage to see, because if you did, that meant you were a prisoner going by, after the battles of December 1917, in the Melette di Foza Mountains. Like Nin Sech, who, before winding up at Mautahausen, saw the roads the Austrians had built, the hospitals and barracks at Camp Gallina, the cable lines climbing Monte Valsugana and the Vezzenes. At Camp Gallina, where it snowed seven months out of the year, they'd even built an all-wood church dedicated to Saint Zita, in honor of their empress. Even the Alpini troops got to build their tiny churches, one right behind the trenches on Monte Luzzo, another at Malga Fossetta, near the hospitals for the men wounded on Ortigara.

The *recuperanti* discussed all these things on their break, and also: "So both our chaplains and their chaplains offered up holy oils and prayed for victory. But they taught us there's just one God. So who's he going to listen to? He probably got sick of it all. 'Go on then—kill yourselves,' he must've said. 'Do what you want. Just figure it out on your own!'" The women and children, picking up the smaller *recupero* the men had left behind, kept working and didn't say a word.

One day when Giacomo's father was digging near an Italian trench on Buso del Giasso, he uncovered the shoes and then, bit by bit, the body of an Austrian soldier, Hungarian, probably, with that name and other information on his dog tags. He'd only just turned twenty when he came all this way, to die in our mountains. He still had cartridges in his cartridge pouches, a grenade and gas mask in his haversack, and a dagger on his belt; in his jacket pocket there was a Francesco Giuseppe medal and a smaller white-metal one of Saint Stephen. And a watch. A heavy pocket watch with a silver chain through the jacket's button holes. Giacomo's father undid the chain. The watch was well-preserved, with a double back and lid; maybe it hadn't been stopped by a bullet, or by the bomb that had killed the man; maybe it had just wound down. He quietly stared at the watch in his hand, then at the body by the Italian trench, the soldier he'd found among the stones. It must have been that night one of their patrols had broken through, when he was on duty. He'd sounded the alarm, yanked the cord to the shelter, the empty cans rattling. Corporal Gigi Frello got there first and manned the machine gun. Then the Campofilon Battery pitched in, too. Giacomo's father sighed. His fingers yellow from the rust, he slowly wound the watch and held it to his ear. It was ticking! He pried up the lid and back with his fingernail and stared at the works running. Slowly, he slid the watch into his pocket, then he squatted and gathered together the other things he could sell, setting them on a rock. Then he started shoveling dirt back over the Hungarian soldier.

Giacomo watched everything, quiet and scared. At one point, his father turned to him: "He was Hungarian. He had a mother, too — and a home where they were waiting for him." Giacomo felt himself choke up with feeling, and he went off a ways by himself. Maybe he wanted to ask something — why was his father being this way? — why the war? But he didn't know how to put it. He didn't talk for the rest of the day.

That evening they came home with a large load of Austrian cartridges they'd found on a rock ledge where some soldier had stashed them fifteen years before. Come winter, when it was impossible to get up into the mountains, they'd empty the gunpowder from these cartridges for the hunters; then they'd remove the bullets, setting them in a helmet on the fire to melt the lead out from the cases; unlike Italian cartridge cases, these stayed all in one piece. Giacomo's mother and grandmother would know how to do all this, too. His father showed everyone the watch and medals that night and explained how he'd found them.

"Our folks who went to work in Hungary were always treated nice," Giacomo's grandmother commented. "Poor Tönle said so, too. This is all Vittorio Emanuele and Kaiser Franz's fault."

His father checked the alarm clock on the shelf to set his watch, pushing the hands to the right hour, the right minute. "In Hungary," he said, "it's the same time as here. I've never had a watch. And look what awful thing has to happen for me to get one." He felt like a thief.

Late one afternoon that summer, an explosion was heard somewhere around Monte Forno. Only the most expert *recuperanti* could tell it wasn't planned, like the bombs they always triggered in the tunnels with TNT. The noise those made was muffled—not like this—not this sharp, violent burst, then afterwards, eerie silence on every mountain.

Soon word got out that two friends from a nearby town had been blown to bits by the enormous mortar bomb they'd been trying to defuse, and the *recuperanti* heard about it, and the shepherds and the cowherds, and the news reached every district—and every house was filled with dread until every member of the family had come home. When they'd figured out who the two men were, the women gathered at the small chapels to say the rosary and the litany, *ora pro eis*, pray for *them*, and not *ora pro nobis*.

All the *recuperanti* went to the funerals; those who'd lived close by the two friends carried the two coffins on their shoulders from the church to the graveyard. The coffins were light: that's because the bodies had been scattered around under the mountain pines, among the rocks and rhododendrons. There just wasn't much left to collect. Not everyone knew this, but those who did kept thinking during the service of how many thousands of soldiers had wound up like that, the word "missing" the last word about them, sent on from Military Headquarters to home. And how many *recuperanti*—and how many to come — would finish up in the exact same way. But no one wanted to admit this to himself: something like this would happen, and they'd all make a silent vow to only go so far, to forget about some kinds of bombs. To stay on their guard even more.

For a few days after the explosion, some of them swore they wouldn't go back to that desperate work. Vu never did quit, though, and he'd tell people that the wise man learns how to be careful at all costs, and — like it says in the Bible — that he's got to hold life in his right hand, and riches in his left.

15

Autumn came early. The insistent rain that always marked the woodcocks' leaving kept the *recuperanti* from going out much. One Sunday afternoon in November, four friends were huddled under Piero Ghellar's cantilever roof. Hands in their pockets, shivering, they watched the sadness blowing gently over the piazza and the streets. A short while before, they'd added up their pocket change.

"Four of us!" one of them burst out. "And we can't even come up with four lire to go to a movie — we don't even have *one* lira to get ourselves a half-liter of wine at the tavern! What kind of life is that!"

"I'm joining the fascists. Then maybe I can get into the border guard."

"You'd be better off trying for the forestry militia," the first one said.

"It's harder to get in," another answered. "You've got to have good recommendations. And there's no telling when those jobs will be posted, either."

"Tomorrow," the first one said, "I'm going to the town hall to see if there's some jobs listed — any job. I can't stay around here anymore. Maybe I'll sneak into Switzerland and find some work, way up in the mountains. Like Toni Ballot did."

"I think I saw a job posted over by the public bathrooms. Let's go take a look."

It was a notice to sign up for two years in the royal *carabinieri* with reenlistment into regular service. The one who'd said he was anxious to leave slowly read the notice aloud. Then he said, "Tomorrow morning, I'm going to the Registry Office to get the forms. I'll sell the *recupero* in my shed to get my papers stamped."

"Not me," another one said. "I'm not going into the *carabinieri*. I'm waiting for the forestry to be posted. And I'm joining the

Fascist Party, too — and I sure hope my pink card doesn't come in the meantime."

That pink card was your draft notice ordering you to present yourself for military service and also serving as a pass from home to your designated barracks.

The four men watched as Albino Vu made his way slowly up the street. They greeted him and asked if he was going to the movies.

"The movies! — what for? — life's one big movie! Last night I was out drinking some and I wound up spending the night at the *carabinieri's*. Good people, them *carabinieri*. So now I'm sober, and I'm headed back to Boscosecco." He stopped and took a deep breath: he hadn't talked that much in a long while. But he'd known these four a long time, since they were kids out hunting with their shotguns.

"There's a good movie playing," said the one who wanted to go into the forestry militia. "It stars a beautiful actress, Greta Garbo. She plays the queen of Sweden."

"I don't care if they're beautiful *or* Garbo — don't you listen to women's garble." Vu shuffled off again, his *recupero* sack over his shoulder.

People said Albino Vu acted that way because of what he'd discovered after he came home from the war: while he was off in the trenches, his girl was fooling around with his friend who'd been rejected by the army. After that, Vu left town, his house, everything, and headed into the mountains where he'd fought and where he'd lost so many real friends. He stayed up there, even in wintertime, in some pasture, or holed up in a bunker, waiting for spring. He didn't need much to live on, almost nothing. He found quality *recupero*, not quantity, and always small stuff: dried gun powder for the hunters that he traded for shoes or old clothes; copper he'd sell to Seber to buy himself just enough food to hold him for a time, and never more than that; the rest he'd spend on wine at Pozza's or Toni della Pesa's where he'd sit and have philosophical debates with Motorcycle Gigi. The four friends watched as Vu walked off, singing a song that cheered up the street.

The *recuperanti* had a crisis on their hands: the lira had been revalued, so metal prices dropped, and even worse: the forestry militiamen and the local woodsmen were saying the *recuperanti's* digging was destroying the topsoil in the pastures and damaging the seedlings so the woods couldn't grow back. Someone informed the authorities, and they threatened the *recuperanti* with fines, even prison.

One day around the summer of 1931, we found out the National Fascist Party was planning to set up an enormous camp, right here by us, for the children of Italians in the Fascists Abroad Organization. They picked a spot in the fertile meadows of the Rendola district, and the hay was cut and gathered early.

"So," the *recuperanti* said, "you get fined for digging up rocks in the mountains. But destroy our best meadows, and you're a hero."

Giacomo's father was curious and went to Rendola one afternoon to get a look at this famous camp for himself. They were marking the spots for the tents, setting up the kitchens, and digging the latrines. He recognized two of workers, and then there were some men he didn't know; maybe they were in the National Security Volunteer Militia and had come up here from the plains.

"Hey, you!" A man wearing shorts and no shirt was calling to him. "You wanna work?"

"Yeah, but not for free."

"Get your jacket off and come here."

So that's how Giacomo's father found work for almost two months. The first thing was arranging the tents in a row according to the blue prints. The entrance to the camp, down a lane off the local road, was framed by two enormous pennants with the tricolored flag and the Savoy coat of arms; all along this lane were still more pennants with flags leading up the gentle slope to the top of the hill, and finally, to a huge portrait of Mussolini with his bald head. The clearing around this portrait would be for camp assemblies, for raising and lowering the flag. One tent could hold maybe twenty kids; there were enough metal-frame bunk beds for a thousand teenaged-fascist *Avanguardisti*. To carry water from the town aqueduct, the men had to build an above-ground piping system fitted to dozens of washtub taps. In other words, quite the job. It was clear right away that Giacomo's father knew how to do this kind of work. And he always went home at night with something in his jacket pockets: bread, quince fruit bars wrapped in tissue paper, *mortadella* sausage. They gave him a big noon meal and a snack at five—a real waste of food—so he brought the leftovers home for dinner.

He'd been working fifteen days when the province fascist party secretary and the fascist mayor, the *podestà*, arrived along with other officials up from Rome, all of them there to see how Camp Mussolini was coming along. Chauffeurs and aides were bouncing around like grasshoppers.

"You're behind!" the party secretary said. "Get going! Get those pine branches up on the arches—and the fasces, too—get those axe blades and sticks tied together! And how about the sentry boxes? The truck will be here tomorrow with the muskets. Have you set up the gun racks? Hop to! Hop to!"

To speed things up (seeing how the volunteer militiamen liked to slip into the tents farthest out for a little nap after eating), Giacomo's father told the director he ought to hire some other workers: "I know a couple of good men. Men who know how to work and to work hard."

"Maybe you're right," the director said. "Bring them around tomorrow, and we'll see how they do."

The next day Giovanni showed up with Moro and Moleta, two *recuperanti*. Between Moro Soll's shouting and Moleta's quieter approach, they got the militiamen going.

The *Avanguardisti* started to arrive by the rack-railway train. "Our fine boys from the Italians Abroad have heard Mother Italy's great voice calling, and they answer with affection. They are coming to the Altipiano from all over the world: from scorching hot Africa and the wintry North, from the distant Americas to our neighbor nations of the Alps. Here in Camp Mussolini, the language of Dante beats a path into every heart. Our Mother Tongue, sweet vehicle of faith and solid fortress of our nation, stands proud among so many exotic languages, enchanting all with her sweet song. As these boys wander our mountains, they will grow to appreciate the beautiful, heroic stories of their fathers, those brave men who volunteered to fight for their country and told their stories in a distant land, among a foreign people, and these boys will come to understand the silent eloquence of their fathers' memories and will be filled with a greater, ever more vital pride in being sons of Italy." And so on.

One day the camp director (who was really a marshal on loan from the light infantry) asked Giacomo's father if he knew how to cook, too. Giovanni automatically said yes, and so he became a cook's helper, along with Moro Soll.

The last of the *Avanguardisti* were there now. The days went by with the bugle call: reveille, breakfast, fall-in, flag-raising, prayers for the king, for Il Duce, for the country, for the far-off families. Songs: "Rising Sun," "Youth." Then calisthenics, close-order drill with muskets, group games for "instilling discipline and order, physical excellence, quick decision-making and reaction time, and for improving all bodily systems." There were also group hikes in the sacred mountains of the motherland, everyone marching and singing:

> We are Fascists from abroad
> Marching fast and proud
> With Mussolini at our side
> We know how to fight
> We know how to die.
> If the reds dare show their snouts
> Smash'em!
> Give'em our heels and fists
> Smash'em!
> Then to show what we're about
> Smsh'em!
> We'll finish 'em off with a club
> finish 'em off with a club!

At that song, Giovanni and Moro shook their heads. "Poor Italy," they muttered.

After evening rations, lowering the flag, and changing the guard at the camp entrance, the *Avanguardisti* were off-duty. They went out in groups in their snappy uniforms, wandering through town, looking to strike up a conversation with some girls, trying to impress them by speaking another language, but always swearing in Italian. Mario and Nino met a few *Avanguardisti* from Casablanca and Salonica, and they and the girls would all wind up having fun together on Via Monte Ortigara.

One morning the local officials and the *podestà* were inspecting the camp and saw Giacomo's father at work in the kitchen, and they protested because "he was a suspicious element—not an official party member." Old Sharpshooter (that's what everyone was calling the technical director of Camp Mussolini by now) told these officials that it was fine by him, that he couldn't care less if Giovanni was a white shirt, a black shirt, a red shirt, or a yellow shirt. Then came the night, after evening rations, when Giacomo's father went off to the Villa Rossi grove with the leftovers from the kettle and almost got himself fired. Once again Old Sharpshooter came to his defense, this time against Father Salsa, the hero-chaplain who had three rows of medals over the red cross on his chest. The priest had joined the camp to carry Faith and Country to these fine lads of the Fascists Abroad.

Giovanni had arranged things with Giacomo and the other local children to make sure any pasta or minestrone left over after rations got back to their homes. The children, crouching in a trench with their pots, would wait for him every afternoon and evening. Father Salsa surprised him just as he was scooping some pasta out from the kettle.

"What's this?—caught you, you thief!—you swindler!"

"Father, sir, this was extra food. Leftovers. They were just going to throw it away."

"Scraps should be saved for the farmer's pigs!"

"But this is still good. Giving it to hogs—that's such a pity. And these children going hungry."

"These children are lazy, raggedy beggars! They're never to show their faces around Camp Mussolini again! They're a disgrace to

Italy! Now — out! — out of here! Scat!"

The children fled, nearly crying, with what little pasta Giacomo's father had been able to give them. Father Salsa ordered the kettle knocked over, and the rest of the pasta spilled into the dirt, then he went straight to Old Sharpshooter: "This has got to stop — our boys from abroad mustn't see them! Shameful! That man should be kicked out of here!"

"That man's worth more than five soldiers. I'll see to it this doesn't happen again."

That night, after Giovanni and Moro Soll cleaned up the kitchen and prepared for the next day's *caffellatte* and cocoa, they went home and decided on a plan. Every evening at the same time Father Salsa ate at the Croce Bianca Inn. Moro would keep watch and at just the right moment, he'd whistle for the children hiding in the bushes. Old Sharpshooter pretended not to notice; so all that month the local children — and not just the children — enjoyed Camp Mussolini's delicious pasta and minestrone. Things went the same the following year.

In the spring of 1932, work started on the *ossario* or "bone" monument. It was going up on the Laiten Hills, east of town, where the bombed-out houses had been left unrepaired. The boys from town used to climb those hills to play, as their fathers did before them.

In the spring, kites would rise in the sky: "dragons," they called them. Vittorini from the pharmacy could make the very best dragons out of wax paper, bamboo slats, and glue; he'd also come up with a type of wooden reel with iron pins that let out or wound the string, depending on what the dragon needed as he soared up above, higher than the larks, the crows, the circling hawks.

Summers, even though the owners didn't like their meadows trampled, boys and girls went up and gathered armfuls of red lilies ("archpriests") before the grass was cut.

In the fall, the Piazza boys and the Uptown boys used to have wars at the very top of the Laitens, on all the rocks from the cannon volleys, which had been piled in one big heap. Sometimes they'd have sling-shot battles with lead pellets for ammunition. Lucky for them, their helmets were Austrian, not Italian.

Winters, they set up ski-jumps on those hills where everyone had first learned how to ski. And that's how Mario broke his arm one February afternoon, making a jump.

It was a summer day when the engineers and surveyors went up the hills escorted by the *podestà* and the fascist party secretary. With their range finders, their tape measures, their theodolites, the technicians got to work surveying, measuring, scribbling. And so, after numerous proposals, offers, conferences, tests, and on-the-spot investigations, the Roman authorities decided that a great monument was to be built and that this great monument holding the remains of our heroes who'd died on the Altipiano (for the country's salvation) would go right here, on our hills of play. To make room for the imperial-style arch, all the quiet cemeteries in the meadows and woods were leveled. Around a hundred workers started in with picks and shovels, digging up the rocks, preparing the foundation, the cement and marble burial niches. Everything dug up was loaded onto Decauville railcarts, then brought down to the meadows near town and dumped, for future road construction.

16

On Saturday afternoons, Giacomo put on his *Avanguardista* uniform and met his friends in the elementary school lobby where their teacher Valentino had them train and drill. A number of other boys were there, grouped according to age. First-Lieutenant Nini was also there in his smart-looking uniform; he'd been hand-picked by his Fascist Excellency, Renato Riccì, to attend a school in Rome. Giacomo had made sure he was assigned to Nino and Mario's squad: they'd all been promised skis and the chance, if they were good enough, to compete in the championships of the national fascist youth organization, the *Opera Nazionale Balilla*. Mario was squad leader.

Their teacher Valentino would order everyone to line up, squad leaders in front; he'd call roll and have them give the Roman salute because, according to the manual, *Physical Education Methods*, "Training must begin and end with the Roman salute in order to give meaning for these young boys to a seemingly meaningless repetitive gesture."

Afterwards Nini had the boys march like soldiers and then, if it was nice out, they did sprints in the courtyard because "sprints and other exercises requiring speed are the most appealing and appropriate for children, provided these exercises do not continue for an extended period." Nini also had them do sprints in cadence, "soldier-style," because the book said: "Running drills must last only a few minutes for these fifth-grade boys as this sort of exercise takes great bodily effort and the utmost concentration. It is therefore extremely tiring…" But First-Lieutenant Nini never worried much about the "few minutes" part—really, the boys had *finished* fifth grade, and the *ONB* ski championships weren't far off, and in Rome he'd learned that "collective sports create solidarity, driving each man to give his all for common victory."

At the end of the training session, the boys would be worn out, not from the drilling but from all those barked-out orders. They were used to running, climbing trees, leaping off river banks, playing soccer with a rag ball, hurtling down the Laitens on skis, digging for cartridges in the trenches, chopping wood—and things like that. Giacomo, from collecting *recupero* with his father, was the fittest of all.

One Saturday afternoon in December, those *Avanguardisti* who'd been chosen (and had the right kind of shoes) finally got their uniforms and skis. Real ash-wood skis with levered bindings, ski poles with leather straps on the grips and baskets to keep the poles from sinking too far into the snow. A black sweater with "*ONB*" written across in white letters, long gray-green ski pants, and a black wool ski cap. Each boy was happy going home that night, his uniform tucked under his arm and his skis on his shoulder. The captain had strongly recommended that they wear their uniforms only for parades and competitions. Their skis, though, they could use whenever they liked.

Each boy prayed the snow would hurry up and come—that night even. And it did snow! Il Duce made it snow! So, on Sunday, not having planned a thing, Nino, Mario, and Giacomo wound up perched (in their gray-green ski pants but not their black sweaters) on the slopes of Maddarello, all three of them ready to try out their skis "on the shining-bright, endless fields of snow"—in the words of the Alpini ski song they'd learned from their teacher Toni. The girls stood watching from the road, Irene focused on Giacomo: he was the best one! At the bottom, when the others did a snowplough or swing stop, Giacomo did a telemark, just like the local champions.

On Saturdays, the *Avanguardista* skiers met at the elementary school, then headed to Bellocchio's field, skis over their shoulder, singing on their way through town:

Vesta's flame
bursts from the temple doors
youth soars
on wings of fire
Duce! Duce!
Who among us fears death?
Who among us denies his Oath?
Raise our swords when you want us to
banners in the wind
we shall march for you!

At Bellocchio's, there was one coach for cross-country, another for downhill and slalom. The bravest of the boys did ski jumps, sometimes reaching up to eighteen meters.

Meanwhile, winter was eating up the wood on the woodpiles and the supplies in the cellars. Those short days lasted forever when you didn't have a job; during the warmest hours of the day, the men sat outside in the sun. They talked about *recupero*, and faraway emigrants, and the war, and sometimes they'd lower their voices and talk about socialism, changing the subject when a child or a woman walked by. News and fliers about the proletariat's struggle against fascism and capitalism arrived along mysterious routes, mostly from France. Once Nin Sech told the men about two anarchist friends he'd made in America, Angelo Sacco and Bartolomeo Vanzetti, who'd been executed even though they were innocent; Angelo dei Micheloni, back from France, mentioned someone who'd escaped off an island, Lusso — or Lussu, maybe — who was already in charge of the Sicilians from Sassari here on Monte Zebio; and he talked about some famous professor, Silvo Trentin, who'd been forced to leave the country. But the comrades fighting the hardest were down in Schio: someone named Blasco who also went by Marchioro or Tresso; and there was Oseleto, and Virubus, and other workers from the Rossi wool plants and factories, all of them struggling to end man's exploitation of man.

One day, Giacomo's father looked around, then pulled a flier from his pocket and quietly read it to the group: in Russia, Stalin had launched his five-year plan for the collectivization of all property.

"What does 'collec-ti-vi-zation' mean?" Moro Soll asked.

"It means, stupid," his brother Toni said, "that what the workers produce off the land belongs to everyone, not just the bosses and the government. There are people now who live off capital interest and the work of others. And they eat white bread every day, and meat every day, and there's always fancy wine on the table. But us—we want a glass of wine at Forts', we've got to think about it plenty. Can the seven of us come up with enough for a liter? Forget it...."

Winter was eating up the wood, but when it snowed more than twenty centimeters, at least there was fatigue duty shoveling the roads to town; the district men would stand in front of the town hall, shovels across their shoulders, waiting for the police chief and Silvio Landi of the technical office to pick who'd get to shovel according to who came next on the list. Some of them would shovel behind the horse-drawn snow plows opening up the provincial road, while others followed the plow clearing the town roads or the one for the road farthest out, which might stay closed even a day or more. One group, supervised by the police chief, would shovel the piazzas in town, the churchyard, the sidewalk in front of the town hall, the entrances to the public laundries, the intersections. For many men, their only pay the entire winter was for these days of shoveling, and with this sporadic work, they could also get some credit at the grocery stores and bakeries. So many—not just the children—prayed for a snowy winter.

In February, school let out for a week while they held the *Opera Nazionale Balilla* championships. The schools were turned into barracks: they took out the desks and crammed the classrooms with Camp Mussolini bunks for lodging *Avanguardisti* from all over Italy. Even Sicily and Sardinia. These championships also brought a few days' work for the men: one group prepared the classrooms and another worked along the main road building pine arches and low snow walls and lining the road with monuments with fasces and portraits of Il Duce, banners on flagpoles, and coats of arms; the men also had to groom the fields for the races and write out large slogans in the snow: "LONG LIVE IL DUCE!," "DUX!," "LONG LIVE THE *ONB*!," "LONG LIVE ITALY!"; finally, the men had to build the award platforms and the seating for the authorities.

During these national games, even our local teams had to sleep at the schools, so Giacomo, Nino, and Mario wound up back in their old classroom from two years before.

The *Avanguardisti* ate their meals at designated restaurants and hotels: *caffellatte* and two rolls in the morning, pasta at midday, minestrone at night. At four in the afternoon, after racing or training, Signor Valentino would give his squads bologna sandwiches. Before the group-march competition started, the boys took an oral exam as part of their overall score: "Who is Il Duce? What's the *Opera Nazionale Balilla*? Who's king of Italy? How many parts to a musket? Name them. Try aiming the musket at that target. Repeat the Fascist Oath."

Giacomo, Nino, Mario and the rest of their squad had already gone four kilometers in the group-march when Valentino stopped them before the final slope down to the finish line; he'd been timing them and said they were going too fast; after a few minutes, he let them go again, but they still crossed the line early and didn't finish in the top ten. "Whoever heard of a race where you have to go slow!" Giacomo said.

Next came the slalom and ski-jump competitions. After their evening meal, during the hour break, Mario and Giacomo went to Gino Soldà's for some fast resin. Soldà lived near Mario, in two rented rooms on the first floor of a house, and that's where he made his ski resin from pine tar, virgin wax, paraffin, and Greek pitch, all melted together in five-kilo pots on an iron stove, the fine smell of pine tar drifting over the street.

"Signor Gino," Mario said, "could I scrape your pots for leftover resin? We've got the slalom and ski jump tomorrow."

Gino Soldà, always kind, laughed and said: "It could come in handy. For how many races?"

Mario called to Giacomo, who'd been waiting outside, and with a broken saw blade they scraped some "Soldà" resin into an empty shoe-polish tin.

"Just wait and see how fast you go tomorrow," Gino Soldà said. "Get a lot rubbed into the bottoms of your skis. But be careful you don't fall."

In the slalom, Mario made mistakes at two gates and Nino got third place, but Giacomo won the "junior" ski jump competition. Then one afternoon before all the *Avanguardisti* returned home, the awards ceremony took place on the piazza platforms, among all the banners and snow monuments. Captain Renato Riccì himself gave out the most important trophies and medals. Giacomo also received a really nice wool sweater and a pair of gloves. And there in the crowd, Irene was waiting for him, so they could walk home together.

17

They were waiting for the spring thaw like they'd never waited before. The larks had returned to the sunny river banks, but since it still froze up here at night, the birds — or so the older people claimed — would fly back down to the plains at dusk. Everyone was waiting, too, for the jobs to start up again and for the time when they could start spreading manure on the potato fields. The Grass family was already hauling manure in panniers, early in the morning, step by step up a path, over icy snow and patches of bare ground: over "*harnust* and *happar*" as they used to say in the ancient tongue. The Grass family was getting a head start on all the field work, making sure everything was done at home in case jobs opened up on the huge *ossario* monument or on some community road project.

And when the late-morning sun was high enough to warm the communal fields, Giacomo and his father would go up with picks and shovels and work their small plot of ground by the woods. Both Giacomo's father and his grandmother thought this plot would be good for lentils, maybe even potatoes the year after that. Twenty kilos of lentils in the house by November meant good minestrone all winter.

They would borrow five kilos of seed lentils from the Zais, who'd had an excellent crop the year before with their big field on Poltrecche; if they couldn't pay the Zai family back in lentils, they'd do it selling *recupero*.

And with winter coming to an end, they weren't the only ones clearing the communal fields by the woods, out past the private properties. In a number of the sunnier spots on the hilltop, smoke rose from the fires of those burn-beating the brush and turf. Glacial moraine and rocks were gathered to make dry support walls for reducing the slope; the rocks and gravel piled up from the digging were placed below these walls. If there wasn't enough manure to spread over their plots, people used beech leaves and red-spruce shavings instead. By the time the cuckoo returned in April, the finished plots would be so neat and orderly, so harmoniously sculpted from the landscape, so breathtaking as seen from Petare-itle Hill, that they'd be called "The Gardens."

With the noon bell, everyone gathered together to eat, to talk a little about life and smoke a pipeful in peace. Gigio Rizzo, the municipal guard, would pass by once in a while to check on their work and to make sure everything was going according to the unwritten laws: no damaging the woods, no trespassing. He also had the job of figuring out the total area tilled by each family for the annual municipal tax on their permanent lease.

Gigio Rizzo was stern but fair, a man of few, but choice words. Always dignified in his forestry uniform and well-oiled boots, carrying that cornel-wood cane with the curved handle, walking with that fast, sure stride; you always felt his presence, even when he wasn't there. He didn't wear a sidearm and if he sometimes heard subversive talk, well, he certainly wasn't reporting anything back to the *podestà*. Like that day Giacomo's father blew up about all the misery and how Il Duce's revaluing the lira and decreasing wages was helping out the capitalists, not the proletarians.

With snow creeping back from the heights, the men started going out for *recupero* again, leaving the women to plant and tend the plowed fields.

And work started up again on the *ossario* monument. The touchy inspector from the public works office was incredibly stubborn about the big white blocks from our few Altipiano quarries—the slightest defect and the marble was rejected. Sometimes the quarry workers tried filling in a chip or flaw with marble dust and putty, but nothing got by the inspector: he'd smash the block with a sledge hammer so it couldn't even be used on some less important job.

The blocks, from quarries sometimes as far as two hours away, were dragged up the Laiten Hills on horse- or mule-drawn carts; the stonecutters would finish the marble up there according to the designs: each block had its number and assigned place in the monument. With levers, rollers, jacks, and tackle, the workers hauled the blocks up to the masons, who set them in place. The construction site was one big swarming, organized ant hill; the foremen paid attention to every last detail; the engineers from Ferlini & Roncato Contractors were afraid of the touchy inspector—he'd pop up silently, bark out a few words, and with a single wave of his hand have whole sections knocked down—they'd been carelessly done—or a block already up there had to be replaced.

One hot, muggy June day, a foreman spotted a worker whose shirt wasn't soaked in sweat.

"You! Yeah, you! Come here. Why aren't you sweating? What have you been up to?—lying around in the shade?"

"I never sweat, Boss. I just naturally don't sweat."

"Bull. Don't give me that. Everybody sweats here. We don't want any wise guys working on our hero monument."

"It's not my fault I don't sweat. My comrades'll tell you. Ask anybody."

"Doesn't matter—you're fired. And remember: 'buddies,' not 'comrades.' Come back Saturday for the rest of your pay."

Maybe this foreman was in such a rotten mood because he'd gone into the work-yard latrine that morning and seen "Death to Il Duce" scratched in charcoal on the planks. As a model for the workers, he pointed out the innocent giant who'd just been discharged from the mountain artillery and who, rumor had it, used to present arms with a 75/13 howitzer barrel. He was strong as a horse, with the spirit of a child; using levers and rollers, he moved solid blocks of marble around like they were pumice stone.

At noon, the workers would find some shade in a ditch or by one of the monument walls under construction; they'd make a fire from carpenters' shavings and set a mess kit on the embers, warming up their soup and polenta brought from home. During this hour break, some of the town boys would climb up the Laitens, maybe to see what their play-hills were going through, but also just curious about all the work. The boys started to know these laborers by name, these men from nearby towns: some were young, almost boys themselves; others were old and gray-haired. Many had been in the Great War, but they didn't seem all that moved to be building this enormous monument for the bones of their comrades.

Mario climbed the hills almost every day; a number of the men knew his family, and one day a group asked if he'd bring them a bottle of wine. There were eight of them, sitting around a fire, toasting some polenta on the coals, and with thirty centesimi each, they came up with the two lire and forty centesimi needed for a bottle of local wine. Mario raced down to his family's shop, bought the wine, and raced up the hills again, knowing the men had to get back to work. This way, they could at least have a couple of mugs of wine in peace.

Later at dinner, Mario's grandfather said, "You should go up there every day at ten minutes to twelve with six bottles in a couple of baskets. I bet you can sell every last one."

And so at the foreman's whistle, Mario would make sure he was up on the Laitens with his baskets and his six bottles of wine. He'd work his way through the groups as the men put their money together for the two lire and forty centesimi. Sometimes when payday was far off, they'd ask for a bottle on credit and Mario, just like his grandfather taught him, always agreed without drawing up a note: the poor don't cheat. When the wine was all sold, he'd sit and listen to the men's stories.

One in particular stayed with him. Nando dell'Ecchele told them how he'd sold his *recupero* one night, then stopped at Margherita's for a glass with Vu, and afterwards, going home, when he was just outside town by the cross, there was this silent line of soldiers on the road right in front of him. The full moon kept slipping through the clouds — it was bright out just then, so he got a good look. The soldiers were pale, silent, walking without a sound — except their sighing. The long line of soldiers was coming from the mountains to the south, marching through the hollow between the hills, and up again, through the Val di Nos, toward the higher mountains.

Other scattered groups of soldiers in single file trickled down from the mountains into the valley. You couldn't see a beginning to them, or an end. Nando just stood there, absolutely still, until the dawn grew light, and the moon went down, and they all disappeared.

"The dead soldiers' spirits," said an old worker who'd been a driver in the war.

"Sure," another said, "but were they Italian or Austrian?"

"I can't remember," Nando answered. "Maybe both."

"You ask me," another man said, "you had one glass too many with Vu. Who knows what that glass was telling you."

"I barely had a drop. A half-liter's nothing split two ways."

"And now," said the one who'd spoken first, "here we are, building a monument for the soldiers' bones. And their spirits, out wandering the mountains."

They stayed quiet until the foreman's whistle called them back. Mario, unsettled, went straight home, without stopping in the meadows, and up in his room he sat at his desk and wrote a poem, long gone now. Just three lines are left:

> In the cold moonlight
> they walk the mountains together—
> the living and the dead.

18

When the bull protest took place one Saturday afternoon after the market stands had been loaded back onto the carts, Giacomo, Nino, and Mario were there with the demonstrators on the piazza. Giacomo had followed the peasants in his area who'd gotten word of the protest. They were in their Sunday best, walking down the road, determined, shouting for others to come join them. They were sick and tired of the Provincial Fascist Breeders Association trying to force them to replace their burline cows with *svitt*, or Swiss cows: burline cows had been in their barns and pastures for centuries and according to tradition, had been brought down from the North when our ancestors first settled in these mountains. The burlina won't damage the grass, the peasants and cowherds insisted, and she'll eat in a straight line, not jumping from spot to spot like the *svitt*—and since she's not too heavy a cow, her hooves don't cut the topsoil, and she'll look for grass in places other cows just won't go. The burlina's a good breeder, too, and safe when it comes to calving; plus, she lives a long time.

For all these reasons which the Breeders Association refused to recognize, the peasants weren't about to give in to the law saying they had to slaughter their burlini bulls and castrate the bull-calves. The Association president and the importers must be in on this together, the peasants were saying.

To make sure there weren't any burlini bulls being bred to the cows, the local forest rangers had been called in, along with the royal *carabinieri*, the customs officers, and the forestry militia; truth be told, though, none of these men really turned out to be zealots; on the other hand, Nane Runz (who'd been hired as a game warden by Commander Colpi, President of breeding and the hunting reserve) was so intolerant, he was downright annoying.

Known for his bravery in the Alpini Assault Units, Nane got his hand shattered when a fuse went off while he was out collecting *recupero*, and it just so happened that our medical officer wound up amputating the hand—the same doctor who'd been with Nane from Monte Rombon, to Ortigara, to Piave. After the accident, Nane joined the Fascist Party as the first step to a cushy job. Then the bull decree went into effect and Nane perched over the districts like a kestrel in a larch tree, and if he saw cows being led to the secret breeding stations, he swooped down on the animals and owners at exactly the right moment. His accusations, his reports, were relentless. The peasants were tired of all this and felt they had a right to choose any bull or cow they pleased. And so word got out about the protest that afternoon in front of the town hall.

Nino, Mario, and the other boys were kicking a ball around in the small piazza when all these people came shouting through the streets; the boys ran to see what was going on and found Giacomo among the demonstrators.

The group was in front of the town hall, chanting:

> Long live Mussolini and our burlini!
> Death to Colpi and the *svitt*!
> Give us our bulls! Give us our bulls!

And the boys, delighted, jumped right in—"Long live Mussolini and our burlini!"—and so it went for quite some time until the prefect commissioner got sick of the ruckus and phoned for the royal *carabinieri*, the customs officers, and the forestry militia, who all came on the run, armed to the teeth. The forestry captain had the highest rank so he took charge and ordered the demonstrators to disperse. But his shouting was no match for theirs. So the prefect commissioner, whose office overlooked the piazza, sent a message boy down with a note for the *carabinieri* marshal, telling him to arrest the most worked-up of the men. But the men went quietly: maybe they'd wanted this all along, being led handcuffed through town, to the district prison, without so much as batting an eye. Like the Risorgimento heroes in the schoolbooks. The children and women followed after, shouting, "Long live Mussolini and our bur-lini!" It was like one big, beautiful open-air theater.

Before nightfall, news of the arrests had reached every district, even those farthest out. Late into the night, the women spread the word of another protest the following day, and most of them were so upset about their men in jail that they didn't get a wink of sleep.

In the morning, women rushed to the piazza from every direction, like on the day of the Saint Matthew Fair. They gathered in a tight group at the town hall, and started shouting for the release of their men and for the right to choose their own bulls. When the commissioner and the town clerk saw all those angry, shouting women, they got right on the phone to the *carabinieri*, the forest rangers, the customs officers, the lower-court judge — this judge thought they ought to call his Excellency the prefect and questor.

The *carabinieri* and forestry militiamen surrounded the women who kept shouting: "Free our men! They're honest men!" and "We fought for Garibaldi! We'll fight for our burlini!" The men started grabbing hold of the women's arms, trying to get them to leave. "Cowards!" the women shrieked. "Get your hands off us! Don't you dare touch a woman!"

Then they shouted that they were going to throw the commissioner and town clerk out the window and tear down the mobile Agricultural Education Office, and the guards raced to block the town hall entrance.

The royal *carabinieri* marshal raised his sword and ordered his men to charge — the women didn't budge. They just shouted even louder: "Long live Mussolini and our burlini!"

And how could the marshal and the forestry militia commander carry out the attack when these women were singing the praises of the head of state?

So the peasants' wives refused to go, and they wound up blockading the town hall. Giacomo, Nino, Mario and all the other boys leaving mass stood shouting right beside them. In the end, after a lot of talk, a lot of phone calls, a lot of meetings at the highest level, the order came up from Rome to release the men, and they went home, their joyful wives crowded around them.

Giacomo followed the group as well. In about fifteen minutes, the excitement and shouting died down, and their victorious homecoming was accompanied by just a joke or two:

"So what did you think of jail?" a wife asked her husband.

"We got our dinner from the Croce Bianca Inn," the husband answered, "and a snack from the Excelsior."

"And it was better sleeping on that jail cot, eh, Bepi?" another man said. "Better than sharing a bed with your wife!"

"Is that so?" said the offended wife. "Well, then you can go sleep in the barn tonight—or go back to jail!"

At Giacomo's house, everyone had already eaten; when they learned where he'd been all morning, his grandmother scolded, "You shouldn't join in things like that—they're not for children. You could have been hurt!"

"Not me. I'm faster than all those militiamen and *carabinieri*. You should've seen it, Nonna! Those women were so mad! It was just like the movies!"

"It couldn't have been a very pretty sight," Giacomo's father said. "But the Breeders Association can't force their bulls on us. The men were right. Still, I'd like to see how all this turns out—justice generally turns a blind eye for those with friends in high places. This year, our cow was bred to Zanga's bull. Next year, who knows?" That morning, with the good weather, he'd brought down a sled piled with firewood from Gluppa Forest. A feast was waiting for Giacomo on the table: polenta on the bread board, boiled *cotechino* sausage, sauerkraut, and bacon.

The story of the burlini bulls turned out just as Giacomo's father predicted. Like it or not, the bulls were all replaced with *svitts* and the burlini bull-calves were castrated. One stubborn peasant, absolutely convinced he was right, refused to give in; he found out that in one of the towns below they were still using burlini bulls, and so he decided he'd buy a bull from Novegno, one that had been declared particularly fit by the veterinarians and the Provincial Economic Council (Bull Department). No *svitt* bull was going into his cowshed: "If this bull's good in a town thirty kilometers away," the peasant told himself, "why won't he do up here in my stalls?"

This peasant, who rented a communal Alpine summer pasture, took the small, rack-rail train down off the Altipiano and climbed back up that night, leading Novegno's bull by the nose. One day Nane Runz the guard, always on the alert, caught the Novegno bull being bred to a burlina cow, and he wrote up his report. The bull was taken away, to be sold off by judge's order at the provincial cattle fair. But our man wasn't about to give in; he filed complaint after complaint, lawsuit after lawsuit, until his case reached the Supreme Court of Cassation, which ruled in his favor, ordering the return of the bull upon payment of the three hundred lire fine for having failed to turn in the stud tax slip. Writ issued November 23 of same year, 1933, Year XII of the Fascist Era.

19

That fall Giovanni packed his munitions case once more to emigrate. The early snow had brought an end to any earnings from *recupero*, and with winter at the door, there weren't any other prospects — except maybe a few days' shoveling for communal services or working on the monuments and arches in preparation for the *ONB* ski championships. But this wasn't enough for six months. And so many were standing in line to get these jobs, it was only fair they went to the men with the most children. What wasn't fair, though — first preference went to those who'd joined the Fascist Party. And Giovanni just wasn't willing to do that. He talked this over one afternoon with the other men of the district, then later that night he discussed it with his family as they sat around the fire.

And so he decided, along with Moro Soll and Angelo Càstelar, to sneak into Switzerland, crossing over Monte Valtellina. They'd heard the Calzi family from the Bald district had a relative in Zurich who owned a large construction business and always had a job for someone from home. Once they got to Zurich, it wouldn't be hard to track him down. In each munitions case with its German inscription, the women packed the usual things: socks, undershirts, underwear, shirts, trousers, a wedge of cheese, and two kilos of bread. This time the men also decided to bring trowels, a wall hammer, plumb line, and level. As for documents, each man had his unskilled-worker identity card in his pocket; Giovanni had his expired passport for France, too, and Angelo, his valid passport, also for France. To buy the ticket to Tirano and for a little extra security money, the men sold all their *recupero* set aside for emergencies to Seber.

They left in the dark, on the first train out. Giacomo, his mother, Angelo's young wife, and Moro's sweetheart were all there, under the station canopy, waiting to say their goodbyes. Cecilia del Moretto, the postal courier, was there to deliver her three sacks to the conductor: the usual letters, registered letters, and packages; and Biondo the Sweeper was there with his heather broom, just like always, waiting for passengers and train to go, so he could clear away anything left on the platform.

Once they reached Tirano, the three got in touch with the men who'd be smuggling them over the border. Giacomo's father knew someone in Madonna, one of his war buddies, who gave the three men a big welcome, then fed them polenta *taragna* and sent them off to sleep in his hayloft.

They crossed the border before dawn. They got on a train in Poschiavo but at the Coira station, the Swiss cantonal police asked to see their papers. The police took them to headquarters and ordered them to open the cases with their odd inscriptions: there was nothing illegal inside. No, nothing against the law but — "Your papers aren't in order," the policemen said. "You don't have work permits, you're not skilled workers, and you entered the country illegally. No one's allowed into Switzerland without a work permit and a skilled trade."

"But we just want work," Angelo tried to tell them. "Just work, that's all. Unskilled — any kind."

"Sorry, you can't stay. We'll have to take you back to the border."

So they had to get on another train, and a policeman rode along with them as far as Chiasso, where he handed them over to the frontier militia. There, a fascist lieutenant preached about how the only reason he wasn't going to report them for illegal emigration was that he felt sorry for their families: he wasn't going to send them to jail, but they were a disgrace to Fascist Italy. Oh, the shame of it! — presenting themselves like that to the world — like bums — for a crust of bread! Why not go work in the Pontine Marshes that Il Duce had finally drained — one of his great successes — or they could go to Cyrenaica, Libya, where he was building such marvelous things!

The lieutenant told the railway militia to keep an eye on these three, and he made them get on a train for Milan. In the enormous

Milan Central Station (dedicated by the king on July 1, 1931), the men were confused and miserable, wandering about under the gigantic vaults, past the enormous windows, down the wide, shining marble halls, with all the people going by, preoccupied and indifferent. They found the third-class waiting room and plunked down on the wooden benches to eat some bread and cheese.

"I sure don't want to go home just to sit around all winter," Giacomo's father said. "I still have my French passport. I speak some French. So what if my passport's expired—they'll let me in. You earn less than in Switzerland, but it's still better than Italy."

"You two go to France if you want," Moro Soll said. "I'm headed home."

And that's what they did. Giovanni and Angelo waited for a train to Modane and Moro Soll took the one to Trieste.

Everyone in the district was surprised to see Moro back. "The others should have come home, too," the families said. "It's too risky."

Giovanni and Angelo wrote from France after a couple of weeks that they'd found work building a dam in Chambary, in the Savoy region, and they would send their first money order by Christmas. Moro Soll wound up joining the Fascist Party, and so he was able to get a job managing the snack bar at Valmadarallo, where there was a ski jump and a downhill course, the same course where Leo Gaspard went over a hundred kilometers an hour with those lead-plated skis of his and the overcoat with the bat wings that popped out like brakes when he got to the bottom. At the snack bar, Moro sold sandwiches, bananas, tangerines, soda, wine, and he'd also arranged with a downtown store to rent out skis and sleds to the tourists who came up Sundays by bus or train.

Sunday mornings, Giacomo was there, too, earning tips helping beginners to fasten their skis or wax them with an old iron. Sometimes gentlemen hired him to give their children lessons; then he'd take Irene to the movies in the afternoon.

Without his father, though, it was a long, sad winter. The sun came up behind Sisemol too late and sank behind Pasubio too soon.

Olga wrote from Australia that she was going to be a mother—maybe was already, with that letter coming from so far away. She said Matteo's job was going well, that they were both happy, that they'd already paid Uncle Nicola back for the trip. And she ate white bread and meat every day because they didn't cost much, and it was really hot at Christmas time—hotter than hay season here. Giacomo knew the seasons were reversed on the other side of the world, but as his mother was reading the letter to them, he couldn't help wondering aloud: "What kind of Christmas is that with it so warm? It was cold when Jesus was born. What's Christmas without snow?"

"Tell me, Giacomo," his grandmother said. "You've been to school. Tell me how it can be summer in Australia when it's winter here."

Giacomo took two potatoes from the basket. "Pretend this is the earth, Nonna, and here's the sun. Okay? So the earth's turning like this and the sun like this. It's not the distance from the sun that makes the seasons change. It's the earth tilting on its axis. Like a spinning top. When it's winter here, it's summer there because the angle of the sunrays changes. That's what they taught me in school."

"I don't understand a thing," his grandmother said. "It's all a mystery, like the Holy Trinity. I only went to school up to the third grade—Signor Piccolo's class. You've had more school. I've only been away from here once, when we were refugees in '16. Such a long trip. Vicenza was so noisy and confusing. Streetcars, carriages, cars stinking up the roads. So confusing."

Now that there wasn't much work to do, Giacomo wasn't sure how to pass the time. Some afternoons he'd go skiing, but without his friends, it wasn't much fun; he'd stop and watch the ski jumping, too, when the local champions came up on sleds for their training. At home he split more firewood than was needed; he cleaned the stalls, fed the cow, even learned to milk her. When there was enough light, he would pull a chair over by the window where his grandmother sat knitting a sock, and read to her out of *Captain Grant's Sons*, the book he'd borrowed from Mario. So for a couple of hours a day, he'd be caught up in the adventures in the Southern hemisphere, along the thirty-seventh parallel. In the evening, after supper, he'd taken to going to the Nappas' stable, to the gatherings there, and he'd find Irene, who was a young lady now, not a child. How wonderful to come out afterward with it snowing. How wonderful having her close, in the falling snow. And how wonderful, too, when there was no snow, and the February sky was filled with endless stars into the night.

At home in bed, his face to the small eastern window, he'd lie awake imagining that sky he couldn't see now through the frosted-over glass, and he seemed to be up there, as if in the book *From the Earth to the Moon*, sailing along with Barbicane, Nicoll, and Ardan inside the aluminum rocket launched from the Columbiad cannon.

20

After the spring thaw, work started up again on the *ossario* monument; Giovanni came home from France with a thousand lire saved and asked to be hired on as a laborer. At first they kept him hanging, then said no. Maybe because he'd tried sneaking into Switzerland and finally made it into France; or because he hadn't joined the Fascist Party; or for God knows what other reason that had made the authorities suspicious. Had they heard about a fine red thread tying subversive Schio to the Altipiano? The Altipiano, with its high migration rate, higher than anywhere — they'd even voted socialist here when there'd been free elections. After they turned him down, Giacomo's father went back to collecting *recupero*, enraged, taking more risks than normal, dismantling live bombs.

One afternoon in May, Mario was going around selling his bottles of wine to the workers when a foreman stopped him and asked his age and if he was interested in a job as a water boy: he'd carry a bucket through the work site and ladle water for anyone who asked. Three hours in the morning, three in the afternoon, nine to noon and two to five: six hours at sixty centesimi an hour. But then the foreman realized Mario wasn't even fifteen — too young to hire.

"I have a friend who's old enough, though," Mario said. "And he's really smart."

"Is he in the *Opera Balilla*?"

"Yessir. And he's a national ski champion, too."

"Okay. Bring him round at noon tomorrow, and we'll see."

So Giacomo got the job. The hours were good — he could still do his morning and afternoon chores. Being a water boy wasn't too demanding. But he had to make sure that the water was fresh to keep the workers happy. Three lire and sixty centesimi a day was nothing to sneeze at.

Though Giacomo didn't know it, the foremen had decided to hire a water boy because they figured too much time was being wasted when the laborers, stonecutters, bricklayers, and carters went for a drink at the mortar tap and even stood around talking sometimes while they waited their turn to fill their canteens.

That year the monument was completed, and the last decorative touches to the base's four shining white walls were finished with bush-hammers. At each of the cardinal points, the helmeted head of an infantryman, sculpted in classical style, jutted out over the portal.

In the Italian cemeteries scattered around the towns and mountains, a chaplain supervised as the workers dug up the soldiers' bodies. The bones were put in small caskets, each man's rank, his first and last name written on the outside, along with any awards for valor. Meanwhile, in some far-off workshop, someone would be engraving this same information on a small marble plaque. The caskets were carried to the San Rocco church and stacked in alphabetical order. Women from the Committee For Honoring Our War Dead made sure all this was done carefully, without any mix-ups. Sometimes members of the dead soldiers' families who'd stayed in touch with the Committee women would arrive from distant cities, from Sicily and Sardinia, from Calabria and Piedmont, to be there when their loved ones were exhumed and lay a flower on the small casket of bones.

When the workers came across a soldier's grave, especially on the battlefields, they'd gather up anything buried with the body: the cartridges found in pouches were sold as *recupero* while other items like small medals, wallets, and pipes went to the chaplain. For an official count of the unknown soldiers in the mass graves, the workers separated the skulls from the other bones and set them to one side. Then all the poor bones were taken directly to the *ossario* and piled together in the designated pits dug out from our hills of play.

That summer something was going on that the newspapers didn't report and hardly anyone knew about. The men working on the *ossario* monument hadn't been paid in over a month; anyone who wanted could get stamps or tokens good only at the small company store; with these, the men could buy wine, bread, sugar, flour, a few other items. An ugly mood had settled over the work site. Graffiti started showing up in the latrines: "We want our money!" and "Down with—" followed by the names of the more ruthless foremen. After a month and a half with no salary, cautiously, quietly, the workers decided to strike.

The night before it was to take place, Giacomo explained the situation to his father, that the men hadn't gotten so much as a lira in over a month and some of the foremen were awful—they screamed insults at the men, worked them like slaves.

"What're you going to do?" his father asked.

"Stay home," Giacomo answered.

"Smart move."

And his father, who was in a bad mood that night, said nothing more about it. He'd found almost no *recupero*—all that digging for nothing. And two hours wasted in a tunnel on Moschiagh, sitting out a thunderstorm.

The next morning, the engineers, foremen, and the touchy inspector got a nasty surprise—the work yard was empty. They notified the authorities at once. *Carabinieri* officers arrived along with police inspectors, possibly from the *OVRA* (the secret police), and they all read the scandalous words scratched on the latrine planks: "Down with Fascism!" "Mussolini the Pig!" "Long live 'The Internationale'!" "Long live Lenin!"

Company representatives told the investigators that they couldn't meet the payroll until the government in Rome sent them an advance on completed work, as per contract. Rome quickly responded that the company would be able to get its money in a few days, at the Bank of Italy. The police insisted on investigating the strike to find the instigators and the main subversives. And top officials decided that the phrase, "Participated in the *ossario* monument strike," should be entered into these workers' criminal records.

A few days later, some new men arrived at the site, and while they tried their hardest to look like workers, they weren't fooling anyone. The time had come to really watch what you said—especially after the general election on March 25—with the fascist ticket getting the majority vote, the local authorities and higher-ups had gotten cocky.

A short while after the strike, Giacomo was called into the office shed. Inside, a kind-faced man sitting behind a desk greeted him with the Roman salute.

"Listen," the man said, "I know you're a fine *Balilla* boy and a ski champion besides. So you must love your country. As you probably know, what went on here was quite serious. Even Il Duce's upset about it: a strike—here!—where our monument's going up for all the fallen heroes who gave their lives for us, for Italy. Now, when you're bringing water to the men, what've you heard? Anything against Fascism?—against our Duce?"

"No, never!" Giacomo was shaking his head. "I don't listen when the men talk."

"Then why'd you stay home the day of the strike?"

"I drank too much cold water the day before and got the diarrhea."

"I believe you. You should never drink too much cold water. You'll get sick. But from now on, you need to listen to the workers, and if you hear anything suspicious, you tell the foremen at once, but no one else. All right?"

"Yessir!" Giacomo said, crossing his fingers behind his back. And before leaving—just as Lieutenant Ninì Duncali had taught him—he took a step back and gave an impeccable Roman salute.

He didn't say a word about this. Not to his father, not to Irene.

21

One evening at the end of May, Irene told Giacomo she wanted to go to the foot of the mountains where her family had fled in '16. They'd stayed in a tiny house in a meadow — Giglio's Meadow — surrounded by alders, birches, and wild cherry trees. For three years they'd lived there, dirt poor, in that tiny house no bigger than a stall. Her sister Orsola had died there, a little girl Irene never knew. Her brother had talked about this place, and so had her grandfather before he died. "I'd really like to see it. How about the two of us going by bicycle one Sunday?"

"We'd have to figure out the road," Giacomo said, "and we don't have bicycles."

"We could rent them from Toni Folo. They won't cost much."

"I'll see what I can find out. I'll ask your father what road to take."

And Giacomo did just that. The road in the best condition went through Costo and Caltrano; then from Caltrano they'd ride to Calvene and ask someone how to get to Giglio's Meadow. But the shortest route was by way of Barental, Granezza, Malga Mazze and Monte di Calvene. The round trip would be around forty kilometers. Renting two bicycles would cost four lire. They decided to go one Sunday in June, taking the Barental road on the way down and the Costo road on the way back.

They went for the bicycles Saturday evening so they could start out early Sunday morning. Toni Folo asked where they were headed and for how long, and from the dozen or so bicycles he had available, he chose two with multiple gears and good tires.

"The roads you'll take are full of sharp gravel," he said. "You'll need good, solid tires, good gears, and good brakes. And I'll throw in a pump and patch kit in case you have a flat. You know how to fix a tire?" he asked Giacomo.

"Sure, I've seen my friends do it. Looks easy."

"So what's below the mountains? You going for fun?"

"We want to see where my family went during the war — near Calvene," Irene said. "My sister died there of the Spanish flu."

"Ah, those were hard times, children — hard times! My family went to Noventa. I was transferred from the Alpini forces to the air force because I was a mechanic. Listen, go slow downhill and pedal hard uphill. Bring the bicycles back anytime Sunday. You can pay me then."

They took five small loaves of rye bread with them, a hunk of cheese, and a little garlic salami. There would be springs to drink from along the way. Barental was cool, still in shadow; they hurried past Luka and the British cemetery. They had to walk their bicycles up Lapide, and they stopped to rest on the stone bench where — so the story went — the Hapsburg Archduke Eugene once sat waiting to go down to the plains. But then the Italian Infantry had arrived.

When Giacomo and Irene reached the Granezza Tavern with its grass enclosure out back, they stopped once more, this time for a lemon fizz. The Pûne sisters ran this local tavern from May to October; after the snow closed the roads, they'd return home with their four cows and two calves. Refreshed now, Giacomo and Irene set off again, pedaling hard for the Granezza Plain. At Mazze, on Monte Boccetta, they could see the Brenta and Astico Rivers, twisting and disappearing into the distance, and the air was flooded with the intoxicating smell of narcissus: the meadows were so white with them, you could barely see the green of the grass. The two stopped and stood there, holding hands, looking out over that new, unknown world — the meadows full of narcissus, the districts farther down, all the red-tile roofs, the distant towns with their bell towers. Maybe those dark spots out there were cities. And far, far away — beyond the plains — what were those hills, blurring into the sky?

The world's so vast, they both were thinking.

"Wait," Irene said. "I want to pick some narcissus for my sister."

They left the bicycles on the slope and climbed to the nearest meadow.

"Pick the ones not fully bloomed," Giacomo said. "They'll last longer."

"I'm picking the prettiest ones that smell the sweetest," Irene answered. "It's all so beautiful!" She threw her arms wide, as if she wanted to hug the world.

They picked two large bunches, and Giacomo tied the flowers to their handlebars with twine; they started the downhill ride to Monte di Calvene. Along the way, they crossed paths with some shepherds who were moving their flocks to the Altipiano, and they stopped to let the flocks go by. The men were from the Dalla Bona family; Giacomo had met them when he'd gone for *recupero* with his father at Blackberry Hills. The shepherds recognized him, too. "Hey there!" Guerrino called. "What're you doing in this neck of the woods?"

"We're headed to Giglio's Meadow. This girl's family was there in '16 — they were refugees."

"We were just there this morning. Now we're making our way up to Peloso Meadow, Reitertall, then Galmara. Little by little. Should take a week. We'll see you later."

And they slowly went by, shepherds and sheep, lambs bleating to their mothers, ewes bleating to their babies. Now and then a sheep or two would stray off the road, tempted by the tender meadow grass, and a shepherd would give a wave or whistle, and a dog would sail off to herd the animals back. The rams stayed in the middle of the flock, and one in particular, his strong, curved horns held high, kept his eyes riveted on the backs of the ewes. Donkeys — jacks, jennies, and foals — were mixed in with the sheep: some of the donkeys carried the new lambs born overnight in Giglio's Meadow in their saddlebags. The strongest donkey carried the kettle for polenta and the flour and salt, another, the tarps and skins for the shepherds' bedding.

When they'd all gone by, Giacomo and Irene got back on their bicycles. At Monte they asked directions, then again up in the Capozz Mountains and up on Malso, too. Finally, past the small valley, they reached the abandoned house where Irene's family had lived. There were still coals in the fireplace from the shepherds, and the house smelled of sheep.

How sad it must have been, this poverty. Their house, the vegetable gardens and meadows of home, forgotten. A miserable fireplace, sky showing through the roof, nettles and brush up to the kitchen door, windows sagging on rusty hinges.

"My nonno said you could hear the fighting in the mountains from here," Irene told Giacomo. "But the neighbors were good people. A lot of them tried to help as best they could."

"They were poorer around here than by us," Giacomo said. "Because rich people own the land here."

"My brother, Matteo, told me he left here to work for the military engineers. He was just a little boy."

They stood quietly, looking around the small, filthy kitchen. They climbed to the room at the top of the narrow stairway; a straw mattress still lay on the plank floor, and from the broken-out windows they saw the mountains to the north, the plains to the south. "Nina and Orsola slept in here with my mother," Irene said. "Nonno and Matteo slept in the next room. My father joined them after the war."

They left for the cemetery, asking directions from some peasants out picking cherries. The peasants told them, then asked where they were from.

"So, you lived at Giglio's Meadow," one man said. "Come. Come have some cherries. We're the Nicolis. Do you remember us?"

No, they'd only heard about the Nicoli family. They'd been born after everyone returned to the Altipiano. Irene explained that they'd ridden down here to look around and to lay some flowers on her sister's grave. The Nicolis remembered Orsola, that she'd died of the Spanish flu, and they remembered Matteo, her mother, her father. They asked after her family, and so they learned that Matteo had left for Australia with his new wife and that her grandfather had died.

"Come back here after the cemetery," they said. "Come have a bowl of soup. We'd love to visit." Giacomo and Irene exchanged glances, then agreed.

They rode their bicycles to the cemetery. They looked for the smaller graves; the children were buried along the wall, in the sun, a row of graves marked by small iron or wooden crosses. On some of the crosses, you could still read the names; on others, they'd faded or disappeared. The children couldn't find Orsola's name — maybe it was covered in grass and wild flowers. So they laid the two bunches of narcissus in the grass and flowers.

"Like soldiers who died in combat," Giacomo said.

It was noon by the time they got back to the Nicolis'. In the big kitchen, there were two extra places at the table and soup to eat and polenta with beans. The Nicolis talked about those times, about Irene's family fleeing to the meadow and the war in the mountains, the British soldiers, the Spanish flu that also took their Caterina. They wanted to know about Matteo, if he was doing well in Australia. Giacomo and Irene felt a bit dazed by all the attention. The Nicolis insisted they take along a bag of cherries.

"Put them in your haversack. Eat them when you get to the top of Costo. It's warm out today."

They gave Irene a bottle of their sweet white wine. "For your mother," they said. "Tell her it's from the Nicolis."

The family stood in the courtyard, waving goodbye as the two of them left. And they pedaled along, not talking, until they reached Caltrano and started the push uphill.

Then Giacomo said, "Good people, those Nicolis."

22

Summer dragged on. After the hay harvest, the first of the tourists arrived; most of them were ill and had come up to the woods to clear their lungs. And, in spite of the sign posted outside town that said no begging allowed, there were always poor people downtown, knocking, begging, at the doors of the houses.

When the soldiers arrived and set up camp or held field maneuvers, children would grab whatever container they could find for the leftover rations, or they'd run errands for a half-loaf of bread: mail a letter, buy cigarettes, carry laundry back from the washerwomen. The enormous *ONB* camps had either closed down or been moved, but the provincial Fascist Party meetings were still held around here. There was always the one world, the official world that ran the communities, the gymnastic exhibitions, military maneuvers, and ceremonies, and then there was the other world of emigrants, the unemployed, the starving; families counted themselves lucky to scrape up two meals a day. In the stores, the bills on the books just kept growing.

Now and then some temporary job helped pay for things like a pair of shoes, a pair of pants, two hanks of wool for knitting a jersey, a tooth to be pulled by the doctor—necessities that otherwise wouldn't have been possible.

And raspberry season started. For two to three weeks, if heavy rain or hail didn't ruin everything, the women and girls would leave at sunrise to gather the raspberries; then they'd bring the fruit to the local distillery, which used them for syrup or resold them to Zuegg of Bolzano.

Carrying baskets and wooden tubs, the women and girls would head for the wide clearings left from the war.

Irene went, too, with her mother and the other women and girls of the area. They'd climb a mule-track toward Monte Wassagruba or Peeraloch, and they'd chat on the way, telling one another their stories and small secrets — there were more secrets to tell while picking raspberries. Sometimes they sang the song about the miner returning from the mine or the one about the young man's house that was full of stones and spider webs but that to his love was a palace with embroidered curtains. The women's serene voices spilled over those places where not long before, the crash and din of battle could be heard, along with the groans of the dying.

Some mornings, a female grouse that was hanging about eating the berries would explode into flight — a jump back, heart pounding — but then the women would sigh and laugh together. When they each had around two kilos of fruit in their baskets, they emptied the berries into the tubs they'd set under the shady fir trees, or in a cool tunnel. They all met by a spring to eat and figure out how much fruit they'd gathered. Old Nina would light her pipe. The girls stretched out and napped for a half-hour while their mothers whispered together about their men or the latest gossip. Sometimes during this midday break, the raspberry women were joined by the *recuperanti* who'd been digging nearby and heard the singing: then the talk grew more cheerful, more lively — the Pûne brothers' bashful, off-color jokes had something to do with that.

Later in the afternoon, the women would head back down the mule-path, their tubs brimming with berries and swinging on the poles they carried between them, across their shoulders. The horse and cart would be waiting for them at the Austrian captain's headstone, and they'd load the day's harvest, then all walk together to the distillery on Via Monte Ortigara, to weigh the fruit and collect their pay. Mario would be waiting for the women, and sometimes he'd ask Irene for a handful of berries. Raspberries paid from eighty centesimi to one lira and twenty centesimi per kilogram. If a girl was quick enough, she could gather ten kilos' worth, and so those ready to marry could buy something for their dowry, hemp or flax, for spinning that winter.

23

Each morning, when there was enough light along the gravel mule-tracks, the silent line of *recuperanti* would climb up to the trenches. The men's footsteps on the stones sent the hares into hiding. The nightjar snickered, then settled down to sleep. Giacomo went, too, with his friends from the nearby districts: the Pûnes, the Grasses, the Vuzes, the Sechs, the Ballots, the Càstelars.

If it was nice out, they'd go as far as the Botte Mine or Monte Palo; if it looked like rain, they stopped sooner. One man would pick a section of trench to start digging, another, a weapons pit; others worked by traces of military camps or batteries. Stooped over, silent, they scratched and dug, studying the ground, paying attention to any small, telling sign: caliber and bomb type, nationality, depth, potential for recovery, casings or cartridges. There was a twenty lire reward—or so the notice said—if someone marked the spot of a body for the military chaplain. Then the chaplain would go and retrieve it. The remains of unknown soldiers were laid in the pile in the *ossario* monument; those that could be identified went into a casket with the appropriate dates. After word spread about the reward, a man would finish for the night and go report what he'd found. The chaplain would jot down the location of the body and arrange a meeting time. But he was often late, or he'd postpone—or not come at all—and he'd only give the *recuperante* ten lire, not the twenty he'd promised. This sort of behavior didn't sit too well: you could lose days of work without compensation. So, in the end, the men just reburied any soldiers' bones they found and said a requiem for their souls.

One morning, Giacomo's father had stopped to dig between two trenches facing Monte Zebio. He was finding a little of everything: cartridges (spent and live), lead shot, bayonets, shards, bits of copper, bones. He was collecting it all in three different piles.

Tired, he got up to roll a cigarette, when he saw a man approaching from Shepherds' Pond, a strange-looking man in tennis shoes, white socks, khaki shorts, a T-shirt, and a straw hat; he was carrying a paper bag in one hand. As he came closer, Giovanni knew this must be the same Colonel Crazy that Giacomo had pointed out to him one day.

For some summers now, the colonel arrived like clockwork to rent a room from the town midwife, Signora Anne. Every morning he'd burst out the door and hurry along Via Monte Ortigara, doing his "gymnastics"—his breathing exercises, his hopping, flexing, and knee bends. If any boys saw him, he'd shout, "Gymnastics! Gymnastics, *Balillas*! Hop! Hop! Jump!"

The boys would watch him, partly amused, partly afraid. He'd go to Martin the baker's for a half-kilo of bread and to Betta del Toi's for a kilo of fruit. Then he continued on with that nervous stride, toward the woods and mountains south of town, to Kaberlaba, Magnaboschi, Lemerle, Zovetto, Cengio. Into the night. Eating just bread and fruit. The children told each other that this was the famous Colonel Crazy who, in '16, had taken his soldiers caught trying to desert and tied them to the wheels of his cannon. That was on Törle, when the enemy had broken through, and the Austro-Hungarians were preparing to march down to the plains and win the war. People said the colonel made his men fire point-blank as the Austrians took their cannons: he fired his pistol at oncoming Austrians and fleeing Italians alike. And that's what drove him crazy.

The colonel stopped near Giacomo's father: "Good afternoon, sir," he said. "Tired? Taking a break? You know, smoking's bad for you."

"And it also keeps you from feeling too hungry or thirsty," Giovanni answered, annoyed, "or from going insane."

"I fired my cannons thousands of times on this mountain," the colonel said. "I commanded the Törle batteries."

"Ah, you're the one who commanded the 149 batteries."

"How'd you know they were 149s?"

"Look." Giovanni held out the butt of a shell. "You tell me."

The colonel took it, weighed it in his hands. "Yep. This one's mine, all right."

"*Was* yours," Giovanni answered. "Now it's mine." Then he said, "I hear you fired a few of these our way."

The colonel was quiet a moment, as though remembering. "Who says so?"

"Listen, mister, I was in that war four years and I saw a few things. And last year a Sardinian officer was here and told me that right where we're standing, our own artillery fired on him and his troops."

"Because they wouldn't advance. I fired short to roust them out of the bunkers."

"Maybe. And maybe you just got your calculations wrong. Would've taken only fifty meters."

"My batteries never made mistakes."

"You listen to me now—in war, everyone makes mistakes. Austrians, too. We found Italian fragments in Italian trenches, Austrian fragments in Austrian trenches, British fragments in British trenches. Going up Colombara—where you can barely keep on your feet—we found Italian infantry bicycles. You commanding officers want to know what really happened—take a few lessons from the *recuperanti* and stop reading that crap in your books!"

"What was your division, soldier?" the colonel said.

"The Sixth Alpini Bassano Battalion."

"Ah! You're the ones who got so chummy with the Austrians the winter of '16 at Grotta del Lago!"

"Yeah, that's right. We called a truce because we had six meters of snow. And the June of '17, we were also the first ones to reach the top of Ortigara. But enough already. Let me work in peace. I don't have any commanding officers now."

Giacomo's father ground his cigarette out on a stone and put it back in his tobacco tin; he took up his pickaxe and returned to digging. Colonel Crazy stood there muttering about each object brought up from the rocks, all shattered by his cannons. When he saw a jawbone with its healthy, white teeth, he picked it up, kissed it, and set it down by the *recupero*. He came to attention, his right hand snapping to the brim of his straw hat; then he hopped away, between the boulders that had been hurled in every direction from the mine that went off June 8, 1916.

That evening, as the men stood at their doors discussing the day's *recupero*, Giacomo's father told them about Colonel Crazy.

"Who knows why he's sniffing around here," Moro said. "Maybe he feels guilty for all the people he killed."

"I doubt it," said Angelo Càstelar, who'd just returned from France. "Colonel Crazy's like all those others who think they're always right, always justified in everything they do. Like Il Duce."

"I once met someone on Zebio," Angelo Schenal said, "who told me he was a lieutenant in the Catonia Company—now he's a station master—and he said that where there's that huge hole now from the mine, there used to be a rock as big as a house that they'd climb up with ladders. From the top you could see the Austrians a few meters below—they were so close you could hear them calling each other by name. So, anyway, the Italians and Austrians were both digging tunnels underneath and filling them with dynamite. The night between the seventh and eighth of June 1916 that lieutenant was just coming off duty on the Little Moon (that's what they used to call that rock) and a group of officers went up to study the planned area of attack for June 10. Then it hit—a storm, some say a lightning bolt, some say the Austrians. Here's what really happened: one of the tunnels—maybe both—exploded while those officers were up there having their look around."

"Some nut was probably testing a detonator," Giacomo's father said.

"They say everybody died," Angelo Schenal continued. "Over a hundred Italian soldiers. And God knows how many Austrians. They're still there, under all the rubble."

"I tried getting in one time," Riccardo Pûn said. "Through a tunnel on the Austrian side. But it was too dangerous—I had to turn back with all the shaking. Must've collapsed by now."

"You know," said Irene's father, "a hundred meters behind the Austrian's front line, in other words, right behind the mine, there's this really deep tunnel and to the right of the entrance there's a tombstone for a captain: *Gefallene Wegen Italienische Mine*, it says."

"But you were in the war, so you must know that by mines the Austrians meant all kinds of bombs and rockets. Ours were launched from the Sant'Antonio Cross. They say a Lieutenant Filzi died there—an Irredentist—the one whose brother was hanged with Cesare Battisti. One day I met some people from Trent who'd come here to set up a memorial stone for him. He was never found."

Some of the children were listening to the men's stories. After a while, Giacomo and Irene went off on their own. The youngest, the smallest, went back to chasing dragonflies by the municipal water-hole or catching the fireflies that had come out now that the swifts were sleeping under the eaves. When the women called the children to bed and the men were alone, they changed the subject. Angelo Càstelar took a piece of paper, folded over twice, from his back pocket; he opened it carefully and read in almost a whisper: the exiles in France from every party had joined forces against the fascist dictatorship, and they were calling on all Italians to do the same.

"So you've met these men?" Moro Soll asked.

"Not directly. I get news and fliers from my comrades at work. And I bumped into Mosè Trip, and he told me about three important anti-fascists in this group who escaped off the island where they'd been deported. And there's the Rosselli brothers, someone named Salvemini, Professor Trentin, here from Treviso, and the Walter brothers from Schio."

"Did you say the Rosselli brothers?" Irene's father asked. "In 1920, the first of the year, a Lieutenant Rosselli brought the doctor here on his sled when my wife was having Irene. He was the one who came up with her name—said it meant 'peace'—which sounded good to me, with the war just over."

Night had fallen; they were lighting the lamps in the houses, and the crescent moon was rising to its peak, devouring the starlight. The men put out their cigarettes and set the butts in their tins.

"So where do we go tomorrow?"
"Same as always — out there, somewhere."
"Good night."
"See you."
"Night, everyone."
"Night."

24

"Now it looks like we have to fight a war to *defend* Austria," Moro Soll said the next evening, picking up where they'd left off. "I was in town buying cigarette paper and tobacco, and I heard Mussolini's moving three divisions up here, to Brennero."

"What, are we crazy?" Angelo Schenal said. "What happened?"

"A few days ago they killed Chancellor Dollfuss, and Il Duce thinks Germany's planning to invade Austria. So we'll have Germans at the border."

"They're all crazy," Giacomo's father said. "They haven't buried the soldiers yet from the last world war, and they're already planning another."

"Mussolini wants to put the fear of God in the Germans," said Tin Grass. "But the Germans have a *Liter* who's gone right to their heads. They're drunk on him."

Nin Sech, who usually just smoked his pipe and listened, now, to everyone's surprise, spoke up: "We'll just have to pin our hopes on Russia. They'll butt heads with the Germans, all right. The capitalist weapons manufacturers have too strong a hold on the German people. But in Russia, it's the working class that's in charge. Seems like all we've known is hunger, poverty, emigration, war. Now it's time to wake up."

The night came to a close on these words, and everyone went home to rest so they could get back to collecting *recupero* the next morning.

That summer, there was another accident. A poor boy from the hills who'd come up here to work for food had been tending the calves pastured on Malga Pozze, between Ortigara and Monte Chiesa, when he found a small bomb in the grass. He picked it up, poked it. The dairyman found what was left of him.

With autumn approaching, the cows were brought down from

the summer pastures and the shepherds gathered their sheep at Basazenocio and Busa della Pesa for shearing and inspection. The bird snares and the few hunting blinds were hidden with green branches; on a clear morning, you could hear the hunting dogs after the hares. The day of the fair, the cowherds, shepherds, *recuperanti*, stablemen, and woodsmen gathered briefly for a friendly glass of wine and some tripe soup soaked with bread. And on that long-awaited day, they spoke of something new, something dark and upsetting: Il Duce had a new law requiring pre-military service for boys eighteen to twenty and ten years in the reserves after active duty was completed. Each and every Saturday. All told, one hundred and fifty Saturdays before going off as soldiers and five hundred after coming home! The men's comments were bitter: "Around here, you're a soldier till you drop!"; "They could pay you at least!"; "Saturday's the day for stocking up on winter firewood." But one of them liked the new law; he could see himself in his uniform and boots, shouting, "Fall in!"; "Forward, march!"; "On the double!"; "Halt!"; "Hail Il Duce!"

Winter came like any other: snow, rain, snow, cold. But this year's was even worse; in many houses now, they put out the fires and lamps and went to bed extremely early—sleeping, you didn't use anything up and you didn't feel hungry. When people gathered together, they started talking about Abyssinia: about the riches locked away in the subsoil and the enormous potential for growing coffee, wheat, bananas, cotton; and they talked about Adua, Eritrea. The oldest recalled the names of townspeople who'd gone down there in 1890 to fight Menelik, under General Barattieri, who lost every battle. So he was replaced by General Baldissera. An old woman would sing: "Oh, Baldissera, oh, Baldissera,/ Those blacks, you better beware of ...." And they remembered this song when the news came out in the *Vedetta Fascista* that Quadrumvir General Emilio De Bono had been sent to East Africa to command all the Italian troops.

Every Saturday, Giacomo, Nino, Mario, Min, Lella, Menta, and the others met for ski practice. They raced each other, making a loop from Folo's Meadows to Barental, with hills up and down along the way. The winners of the provincial competitions would participate in the national championships in Piedmont or Vatellina. Usually Rizzieri beat everyone in cross-country, but he was too old now for the *Avanguardisti* and would be racing with the *Giovani Fascisti* instead.

In social studies and Italian class, the teachers were lecturing on East Africa and our army transporting troops and supplies through the Suez Canal.

Giacomo, Min, Nino, and a few other *Avanguardisti* were picked for the National *ONB* championships. They came home with cups and medals; the cups wound up at the local fascist headquarters in Vicenza, but that didn't matter; the personal prizes were better, anyway: sweaters, gloves, skis, long wool socks. When he returned, Giacomo told Irene and Mario everything he'd seen: this was his first time far from home and his first train ride. He ended, though, by saying it was better here than anywhere else.

In the spring, when work started again on the *ossario* monument, Giacomo showed up and a foreman told him he was free to go — a boy from a large family had been brought to their attention by the political secretary, and he'd be taking over the job now. So Giacomo went back to collecting *recupero* with his father. During that difficult time, there were people who couldn't afford anything but plain polenta, and then every three or four days, while they waited to sell their scrap metal, they'd bleed their cow where she stood in her stall, then cook the blood with an onion; snails were good by May; after that, polenta could be eaten with blueberries, strawberries, and raspberries. A trapped hare was cause for celebration. Many of the boys caught birds with lime or slingshots, and for some families, this was the only meat on the table.

Like always, the *recuperanti* gathered together at noon and toasted their polenta; they even managed a joke or two about their misery. Mario Ballot would imitate Il Duce's speeches that they heard over the radio loudspeakers and even the most tight-lipped couldn't keep from laughing. One time he decided to count the total number of patches on his uncle's jacket (seventy-two). But

they all had shirts, britches, jackets, and socks mended with patches and more patches mended with other patches. And their hands and their clothes and sometimes even their faces were yellow — from the pertite and other explosives.

25

Those were bitter years to live through. Some of the large families who'd gone south to work in the drained Pontine Marshes reported back that conditions there were extremely difficult. The word was out that Mad Toni had left the French mines still owing on supplies because the company wasn't paying its workers according to their contracts. Toni slipped onto a freight train with his wife and four children and left a note in the shack for his creditors: "I still owe you, but my little ones need food. You want your money, get it from the mine owners."

At the border, Toni asked to speak to the frontier militia consul and told him he'd reentered the country because Il Duce needed all available hands—he was ready to go to work in the marshes. They gave him a voucher for a meal in the railway cafeteria and travel orders for home. When he reached town, he went directly to the *podestà* and the political secretary: "In France, the people at the Fascists Abroad told me there's work for everybody in Italy. So here I am. My whole family's ready and able to go to Littoria."

But no, he couldn't go—his boys were far too young, not up to working the land. So Mad Toni took his two older sons and headed for Ortigara, to collect *recupero*. They lived in a tunnel; and right there on that mountain, the oldest blew his hand apart with a detonator. Toni bandaged the hand as best he could and rushed the boy to the doctor—this doctor was new, though, and reported Toni to the *carabinieri*, who wanted to arrest him for injuring his son and for embezzling goods of the State.

"Fine, put us all in jail," Mad Toni said. "Then at least we'll get something to eat." He went back to collecting *recupero*.

One day toward the end of summer, Giacomo, his father, and the other *recuperanti* sat having their meal on the slopes of Zebio. It was drizzling rain; fog rose from the valley and hung on the trees;

they all felt wet to the bone, and cranky. It seemed like a late-fall day, not the end of summer. Even Mario Ballot wasn't much interested in joking, though he'd recently worked out some Hitler imitations, a new language crammed with consonants, a few shrill vowels, and some dialect thrown in for good measure. He'd perch on a rock up above and end with the Nazi salute — "*Heil Shitler!*"

But this wasn't the right day: the tedious, insistent rain sure didn't make them want to dig for very long in the trenches. They just sat there, silent and miserable. Then all at once, Meneghin Picche hurled his pickaxe, shouting, "I'm sick of this life! Enough already!"

But who knows how he thought he might change it, or even what he'd had "enough" of. The pick bounced and made a strange noise. Picche, usually so quiet, seemed a bit sheepish after this little act of rebellion; he went for his pick, and under his feet, there was that same noise, an empty sound. With the flat of the blade, he scratched at the ground, and some wood planks surfaced; he pried up a couple: a crack showed in the rock. It was crammed full of Italian cartridges.

"Come here, quick!" he shouted.

Mario Ballot, Nin Sech, Moro Soll, Angelo, Giacomo, and his father stood and stared in amazement at that sight — a treasure chest — and God knows how it got there or why.

Meneghin Picche started scooping out great handfuls of cartridges. They seemed to go on forever. Live, in perfect condition, which meant powder for the hunters, too: lead, brass, and now even powder. He'd gathered a nice pile, a rough guess, maybe two hundred kilograms — and he still hadn't pulled them all out by dusk. Meanwhile, his friends were musing on how the cartridges got there in the first place; they kept looking back and forth, from this dugout just behind the Italian trench, to the Austrian trench across the way. Maybe it had been a saboteur; or some soldier wanting a nice bonus at the end of the war; or a revolutionary putting together his stockpile. But it was Giacomo's father, with all his experience, whose guess seemed most likely:

"You see that overhang in front of us?" he said. "That was probably a Fiat machine gun position. And behind here, in this shelter, this must be where the munitions carriers had their cartridge supply cases for refilling the clips. In November of '17, when the order came down to retreat toward the Melettes and Monte Fior, they couldn't carry everything. To keep the Austrians from getting the cartridges, they must've hid them in here." And then he added: "For Meneghin Picche, who was sick of digging up *recupero*."

The next day, they came back with Nappa's horse and cart. Meneghin kept scooping out cartridges until noon, and afterwards, they helped carry them to the mule-track. By the time he'd piled them all into his shed that evening, there looked to be about seven hundred kilograms. He and his wife spent another fifteen days emptying the powder, and when he sold the *recupero*, his family had enough to live on all winter. And even some for the winter after that.

The nice fall weather returned, the horizon clear, the sky bright. On October 3, 1935, Nino and Mario decided, as they had so many times before, to go to Rasta's bird snare in the afternoon. The chaffinches were migrating, and if the boys ate quickly, they could hurry and get there in time to help catch dozens of birds. Then at the end of the day, they'd gather the bird-seed decoys around the shed and fill the water troughs in the cages.

But no, that's not how it went, because before noon, the school principle had the janitor go around to the classes and tell everyone to put on their uniforms and meet at the town-hall piazza: Il Duce was about to make an important speech on the radio.

So many of them in one place: militiamen; *Balilla* boys, *Avanguardisti*, and *Giovani Fascisti*; girls of the *Piccole* and *Giovane Italiane*; and women of the *Donne Fasciste*. Then in front: the *podestà*, the political secretary, the teachers in uniform, the *carabinieri*, the customs officers, the forestry militia. "All hail Il Duce!" Achille Starace shouted in Rome, his voice blaring by loudspeaker to all the piazzas of Italy. "Hail Il Duce!" the crowds on the piazzas answered back.

A strange euphoria welled up in the children, the teenagers, and even in the adults as they listened to Il Duce's words — "Du-ce!

Du-ce!"—the crowd kept interrupting. The time had come, he was saying, to avenge our heroes at Adua, to right the wrong in Ual Ual; and at this very moment, even as he spoke, our valiant troops had crossed the borders into Ethiopia, utterly, unshakeably confident of victory. "Du-ce! Du-ce! Du-ce!"

Late into the night, the streets of town were strangely alive, filled with groups singing patriotic songs and songs of revolution. In reality, few, very few, were upset.

Giacomo's father was one of them. The next day he and his son went looking for *recupero* by Columbis' Cave. They were digging in front of the Austrian positions, with their two barbed-wire entanglements, when they heard the Müllars' hounds. By now they could tell those dogs apart as their voices rose in the valley: Cimbro, Selva, Bosco, and Stéla. The dogs had picked up a scent here and there in Kemple del Passo Stretto before the sun had even touched the hoar frost. Selva crisscrossed back and forth until she found the right scent and flushed a hare from its nest. With Selva's first yelp, then her joyful barking, the three other dogs stopped searching and raced after her. Their voices echoed through the valley. Cimbro, the aggressive one, took the lead, hurdling the others, off and running on the trail. His confident baritone made the waiting hunters feel confident as well. Bosco was more of a tenor, clear and sonorous; the rocks of Piandot sent his voice bouncing back to Colombara; and Selva and Stéla sang a sharp, happy counter-melody, and the whole valley rang.

Must be an older hare, Giacomo's father thought, since they haven't caught it yet.

The dogs' barking was swallowed up in the Fiara and Mandrelle woods, resounded in Boscosecco, and on Fontenello, there came a shot, then a drawn-out "Gaawt iit!"

The barking stopped. By now it was noon, and Giacomo and his father set off for Fontenello.

The four dogs lay sprawled asleep under a big, shady fir tree; hanging in the branches above their heads were two hares instead of one. The three Müllars sat eating polenta and cheese near a hollow tree trunk full of water.

They all greeted each other and then: "So you were out hunting today," Giacomo's father said. "But I only heard one shot, and I see two hares."

"Well," Tan Müllar said, "Selva happened to stay behind, and she found a second one at Ramstone, and it ran toward me. I was by the Buse Magre pasture, so you wouldn't have heard my shot."

"You had yourselves a good day then."

"And how about you?" asked Giovanni Müllar.

"The usual. Enough to eat on."

"Better here in the mountains than in the piazza," Valentin said. "After Il Duce's speech yesterday declaring war on Abyssinia, folks were up barking all night."

"It was bound to happen sooner or later," Giacomo's father said. "But sometimes a man'll light a fire and not know how to put it out. And money's not the only cost in war. Just look around. We're still finding the dead up here."

"The newspapers keep saying Abyssinia's got everything," said Giovanni Müllar. He started counting on his fingers: "Gold, oil, iron, coffee, land ripe for growing."

"But if it's got so much," Tan wondered out loud, "then why haven't the British or French taken it themselves?"

These were the plain words that day of three hunters and a *recuperante*. Giacomo stayed quiet and listened and didn't know what to make of it all.

26

On October 7, the headlines read that Adua had been retaken. The Ministry of Press and Propaganda sent out the following: "Communication no. 14: Eritrean Front. This morning, October 6, troops of the Second National Army Corps continued their advance at dawn. By 10:30, they entered Adua. The authorities, the clergy, and much of the general population were present at Headquarters for the act of formal surrender."

In social studies, the teacher called Mario up front and had him pin tiny tri-colored flags on the map of East Africa, on Adigrat, Entisciò, Adua, Abba Garima. In Catechism class, they talked about Father Reginaldo Giuliani, gold medal for military valor, a fallen hero who died beside a machine-gun, fighting off the barbaric Abyssinian hoards; the music teacher had them sing "Little Black Face." At home, people talked about the Pusteria Alpini troops defeating the Imperial Negus Guard at Mai Ceu. On November 18, The League of Nations imposed "unjust" economic sanctions on Italy, and children in the fascist youth groups, the *Balillas*, *Avanguardisti*, the *Piccole* and *Giovane Italiane*, were sent out to collect anything metal found in the attics, as well as copper pans from the kitchens, and, around here, the brass shell casings that everyone used for flower vases. All for Country, for ammunition, weapons, ships. And there was gold for Country, too: on December 18, at the altar of the Unknown Soldier, the Queen gave up her wedding ring, and every wife in Italy followed suit.

Under the sway of all this emotion, Mario wrote a letter to Il Duce asking to go fight in East Africa. He could march long distances, he knew how to use a musket and, if necessary, he knew how to use his fists.

It wasn't long before he got his answer. A letter arrived, right at the house, a heavy, white, fancy envelope and then, on official letterhead:

"Commander of the *Opera Nazionale Balilla*: Dear *Avanguardista*, your devotion to the Fascist Cause, your act of ardent patriotism is much appreciated by Il Duce, and he has directed me to send you his highest congratulations.—Renato Ricci."

And in recognition: "an *ONB* merit cross." Mario's grandfather was the only one who made fun of all this: his father was so proud, his mother astonished and afraid, his friends a little jealous of his bravery. But not Giacomo. No, Giacomo just told him he was nuts.

The price of scrap metal doubled in the next few months—copper was up to five lire a kilo. But with all the snow that winter, there was no getting into the mountains; when the dark, thawed spots started showing in the pastures, the *recuperanti* were right back at it. As the snow retreated up and up, the men would follow.

The summer of 1936, there must have been over a thousand people digging in the mountains, and many stayed up there for weeks, sleeping in bunkers, in Alpine summer pastures, in the shepherds' huts. And the number of accidents increased: to make any money, you had to take more risks; no one ever heard about the less serious incidents—the newspapers didn't even report those that were fatal. The local doctor patched up the wounded like he'd done in the war: a shot of morphine, a quick exam, a dressing slapped on; then load them into Vittorio's hired car and get them to the hospitals below.

On the evening of May 9, the Empire was proclaimed. All over Italy, the piazzas were jam-packed, everyone overjoyed, ecstatic, singing Il Duce's praises. They listened, completely silent, as Mussolini spoke, until the end: "This Empire was born," he shouted, "from the blood of the Italian people. Now with their hard work, they will make it grow, and with their weapons, they will guard it from all enemies. Be supremely confident in this, Legionnaires, and raise your flags, your swords high; lift your hearts, and after fifteen centuries, welcome the Empire back to the Roman Hills of Destiny. Are you worthy? Your shout is your sacred oath, your pledge before Man and God. Through life, through death. Blackshirts, Legionnaires—Hail to the King!"

That evening, a resounding cry of agreement rang out, but there were so many poor people, so many emigrants, woodsmen, *recuperanti*, and laborers who weren't in the piazzas shouting. And around these parts, two brothers, two cobblers in *Giovani Fascisti* uniforms, were riding their bicycles down to Schio, where some comrades gave them fliers, underground anti-fascist propaganda, that the brothers carried back to the Altipiano and handed out in the poorest districts. Once read, the fliers were stashed beneath the wood piles.

27

The great *ossario* monument was nearly finished. One by one, all the caskets of soldiers' bones had been slid, in alphabetical order, into niches along the wide halls. On all four sides of the Roman arch, a Winged Victory statue stood in her nook, holding her torch and fasces. The scaffolding was gone now, the last workers dismissed.

These days, around here, if you didn't have a steady job, you either joined the hundreds of workers going off to East Africa or you joined the *recuperanti*. Italy was crying out for metal. Four times a day, the rack-rail train left the Altipiano, its three uncovered cars piled high with scrap weaponry to be melted down in the plains' foundries for more weapons, more ammunition. Meanwhile, yet another war had started in Spain.

Some of the *recuperanti* who'd fought in the Dolomites in '15 and '16 decided to take a look around Cortina — word was, this area hadn't been picked clean yet. Giacomo and his father left with Bepi Pûn, Moro Soll, and Angelo Càstelar. Hauling rucksacks and tools, they reached the Falzarego Pass after two days' travel on foot and by country bus, and near the Lagazuoi Mountains, they found an Italian barracks that had been abandoned in '16. This became their base.

They left the next day at dawn for a week of exploring along the Italian line that made a semicircle from the Pass to Piccolo Lagazuoi. Continuing on, they reached Falzarego Peak, Travenanzes Fork, Col dei Bois Fork, and finally, Castelletto and the slopes of Tofana di Roces.

They'd return each night to the barracks with a nice load of cartridge cases. The second week, they explored the Austrian line from Stria's Rock, around Grande Lagazuoi, to Torre di Fanis. And all along the way, they found live and spent cartridges by the rifle and machine-gun positions. Once these places were cleaned out, they set to digging near any signs of bombing—there were countless 75 and 149 shrapnel shells, lead balls sprayed all around the bomb craters.

Sometimes Giacomo would stop and admire the strange, wild landscape. At night, it was fascinating to see the rocks go from red to violet, especially on Torre di Fanis and Tofan di Roces. He wished Irene was with him then, and every evening, with the first stars over the silent mountains, he'd tell her goodnight.

Day by day, they were accumulating an enormous pile of *recupero*, two truckloads at least. They made a deal with a buyer from Pustertal, a better offer than any they'd get on the Altipiano; but the day before the sale, two *carabinieri* showed up with orders to confiscate the lot: someone had reported them to the Cortina *podestà*, who'd notified the *carabinieri* marshal. It was the first time war materials had been collected in these parts—they were still considered State property—and the buyer, Ploner, arrived the next day with two trucks, and he had Giovanni get in his car, and they drove straight down to the *podestà* at Dobbiaco.

At one point during the conversation, Giovanni said, "They tell us to stand on our own two feet, to buy Italian, that saving's important. Then they confiscate our *recupero*, even with Italy needing metal so bad. Besides, if we don't get it, isn't this stuff dangerous, just lying around in the mountains?"

The Dobbiaco *podestà* had to agree with him. And since part of the *recupero* was in his municipality, he made a couple of firm phone calls, then he told Signor Ploner, "By all means, go ahead and load your trucks."

The next two months they were left to work in peace in the Falzarego area; then they moved over to Valle Popene for nearly three months, using the same methods that had brought them so much luck in the Lagazuoi Mountains. And everything found on Popena Alta, on the slopes of Cristallo, on Monte Piana, they'd carry just over the Marogna Bridge, into the Bolzano Province—to keep the Cortina *podestà* off their backs. And every week, Signor Ploner came by to load up a truck.

In the crags of the rocks, Giacomo found Austrian and Italian coins and medals of Frans Joseph and Emperor Charles; there were also pipes and rosary beads in the trenches on either side. One difference from the Altipiano—no dead bodies around here. Maybe there'd been time enough to bury them. In the most unexpected places, in tunnels along the ledges, they found piles of uniforms and shoes, all useless now. A shame.

On September 18, they sold their last load. They were homesick by now, and they were dying to wash off all the yellow from the explosives. At a tavern in Carbonin, they treated themselves to a dinner of roe-deer meat and polenta, and by the night of the twentieth, they were all back home again, with a nice little nest egg that would certainly hold them come winter. That very same night, Giacomo went over to visit Irene.

28

The Saint Matthew Fair filled the streets and piazzas of the main town with splendor. People were hurrying in from all the surrounding hills and villages; the horses pulling two-wheeled carts had ribbons in their tails. Before reaching the fair, many of the women, their feet bare inside their clogs, would duck behind some corner to pull on stockings and shoes. The horses, the cows, the sheep, the pigs, the chickens were all kept in the meadows nearest the center of town; the tables where the farmers did their business were full of farm implements and forestry equipment, full of harnesses and ropes. And every year, the phony German would be in his same spot, selling his razor blades and sharpening stones for knives and sickles.

He'd shout in German, praising his goods spread out on the counter, and he was always dressed like someone from Tirol, a pheasant feather in his cap. "I coming from Solingen like ze zings zat I selling," he'd say. But Mario had heard him whispering in perfect Bassa Veneto dialect to his buddy while the farmers crowded around them. He'd make everyone gasp (and make quite a number of sales) as he chewed razor blades in their wrappers or snapped glass in his teeth, the same glass he normally used for demonstrating his high-quality millstones, like a glass-worker makes use of diamonds. One time he found himself in a bit of a tight spot when an emigrant started speaking to him in real German, but he managed to distract the guy by offering him a packet of real Solingen razor blades.

A little past the phony German was the bookseller's stand, owned by the Tarantola family from Pontremoli: a father, mother, and daughter. They'd arrive the night before the fair with a cartload covered by a large canvas tarp. A little white pony pulled this heavy load, but in the long climb up, they'd have to help push.

Giacomo and Mario caught sight of each other and called back and forth through the crowd. They lost each other, found each other.

"I haven't seen you in months. Irene told me you were collecting *recupero* in the Dolomites. How'd it go?"

"Really well. We found a lot, and the pay was good. And those mountains, up close! There were times, at dusk, they'd turn red, then violet. But it was dangerous, too. Some places, we had to tie a rope around us that we bought in Dobbiaco. Look — this is for you — I found it on Monte Forame."

It was a medal of a young soldier in profile with an inscription running round the edge that Mario sounded out: "*Ca-ro-lus I D G Imp Aus Rex Boh et Rex Apo-st Hunng.*" He turned it over: a laurel trophy and some flags surrounded the word, *For-titu-dini*. "Thanks," he said. "Must've been an Austrian soldier's. I think it's in memory of the last emperor, Charles."

"Hey, Mario, listen. I've got twenty lire here — I want to buy a present for Irene. I was thinking maybe a nice silk kerchief."

"No, don't get her that. Handerchiefs are supposed to bring bad luck — they're for drying tears. Let's look around some. Is Irene here?"

"She's with her mother at the fabric stands."

"If you want to surprise her, we have to make sure she doesn't see us."

They walked through the market, asking prices, not able to make up their minds. Finally, Mario convinced Giacomo to buy a blue wool shawl with white fringe.

"When it's warm around her shoulders," Giacomo said, "she'll think of me."

"I've got two lire to buy some books. Let's go."

They pushed through the crowd around the most mesmerizing of the merchants, and they reached the Tarantolas' book stand. The books were carefully arranged: fairytales, adventure and travel books, romance novels, historical novels, epic poetry, detective novels, bargain books, and even foreign-language dictionaries.

They looked through everything, then went back to the adventure books. Mario was having a hard time deciding between *Michael Strogoff* and *Robinson Crusoe*; each was over two lire—he'd have to ask his mother for another thirty centesimi. But that set, *Italian and Foreign Writers*, edited by Gian Daùli, was fifty percent off, so he could buy two books. But which two? Mario picked up this book, that book, flipped through them, read the covers, put them back. The Tarantolas let him do this—they knew him from past fairs.

"Come on, hurry up," Giacomo told him after a while. "I have to meet Irene and my father over by the pigpens."

Mario finally chose *The Jungle Book* and *The Call of the Wild*. "I'll loan them to you when I'm done. They should be good."

He even got twenty centesimi back from Signora Tarantola. "Buy yourself some grapes," she said. They bought two bunches of American grapes from Betta del Toi.

By the livestock, horse dealers were pointing their long whips at flanks, hocks, chest, and neck; if someone looked interested, they always pried open the horse's mouth to show the teeth. Now and then the dealers would separate one out from the others, and they'd bellow commands and snap the whip as a stable boy led the horse by the bridle, up and down, in a walk or trot. Meanwhile, off to the side, the middlemen were trying to bring buyers and sellers together, whispering in one man's ear, pulling someone by the arm, pushing two men to spit and shake on it. Past the horses but before the sheep guarded by dogs (while the shepherds were off celebrating the day, as always, at the trattoria), were the fattening hogs in pens and the suckling pigs in big woven rush cages. This was where Giacomo and his father had planned to meet.

Giovanni was negotiating with the dealer from Thiene for the pig that had caught his eye. He'd made an offer of a hundred and ten lire, but the dealer wanted a hundred and thirty; of course they settled on a hundred and twenty. "C.G." was written in blue chalk on the pig's back. "He's a little thin," Giovanni whispered to Giacomo, "but a nice, healthy pig—good and long. By Christmas, he'll be a hundred and twenty kilos easy."

Irene and her father had shown up to buy their pig, too. They chose theirs together, from a dealer who insisted all his stock came from the pig keeper at Poselaro Field.

Irene also had some hemp-cotton fabric in her purse, and she waited for the right moment to whisper in Giacomo's ear: "My mother bought me some cloth for sheets. She said you should buy things for your dowry a little at a time so you don't notice the cost, and then it'll be all ready by the time of the wedding."

Mario heard her, too, and watched Giacomo turn red as he told her, "Here, this is for you."

She ripped open the package with the shawl. "Oh, how pretty! But it must've been expensive! You shouldn't have" — with the shawl already around her shoulders — "It'll keep me nice and warm this winter. It's so pretty! Thank you."

The pig-dealing all taken care of, the two fathers invited the three young people to "Margherita's Place" for a bowl of the traditional tripe soup. Mario thanked them, but his family was expecting him for their midday meal. He'd have to meet them later.

Back home, he found a surprise in the courtyard: two snow-white lambs bought by his uncle, who'd just returned from America. The fleeces would make a nice warm vest before winter, and there was also the meat, of course, to go with polenta.

Mario set his two books in his room, ate quickly, then ran back to the fair to find his friends. He went past the swindler pulling his sleight-of-hand tricks with the guards off at lunch, past the stand of useless goods where a barker stood with a snake wrapped around him. He took a quick peek at the miraculous marmot ointment stand — there was even a live marmot in a cage on the counter. He thought Giacomo and Irene might be waiting for him at Margherita's, so he hurried, but they'd already left.

Silvio Scelli was there, though, in the crowd of customers, playing his old accordion and singing the song of Adua to earn a bowl of tripe soup:

We've retaken Adua
We took back the prize
We've retaken Adua
Now let heroes rise
Fly, Victory, Fly
Let the world hear our cry
We've retaken Adua
Shout 'Hip hip Hurrah!'

Mario caught up to his friends where they'd bought the pigs; they were just taking the animals from the pens, getting ready to leave. He walked with them as they headed home.

Along the way, they ran into Matío and Bepi, who were discussing the unusual rise in the price of sheep and wool. "It's a bad sign," Matío was saying. "The Dalla Bona and Ava families told me the Marzottos and Rossis paid over list. And they think prices'll go even higher."

"Maybe because Mussolini and the Germans are about to go to war. So we should hold onto what little we've got."

"Yeah, if you don't need the money, sheep'll be like gold."

"But remember the old saying, Bepi: '*Ist pezzort lazzen de bolla, bedar de oba.*' It's better to lose the wool than the sheep."

"Now just look at these beautiful pigs," Bepi commented as the animals went by. "Nice and long! They'll fatten up good. How much they cost?"

"Mine was a hundred and thirty and Giovanni's was a hundred and twenty."

"Fine fair today," Matío said. "But not much money out there. And everything's so expensive these days. Blame it on the war in Abyssinia."

They were up in their hills now. From time to time, the pigs would stray off the road into the meadows, and Giacomo, Irene, and Mario would chase them back with a stick; the four men walked behind, talking about prices, and crises, and jobs. From the bell tower, the six bells rang as one, and "*Ad onorem Sancti Mattei apostuli et evangelistae*" spilled over the houses, the meadows, the woods, and the work of the people.

29

One afternoon, Giacomo's father said, "We can't work six months then sit around here six months staring at each other."

"So what do you want to do then?" Moro Soll said. "You've got to wait out winter. Just like the badger."

"Oh, sure, that's easy for you to say. You have the snack bar at Maddarello, so at least you're earning something. But what about us?—and all the others?"

"Oh, you can all go hang out at the men's club," Moro joked. "The *ONB* men's club. But there's Nin, you know, who hasn't joined the Fascists—he's a comrade—and he's managed to buy nine sheep."

"Yeah," Giacomo's father said, "and he's also got hay—sheep don't eat snow. Tomorrow I'm filling out the forms to work in Abyssinia."

He left in January, along with Angelo and Cristiano.

His leaving wasn't particularly noteworthy. Everybody in the area, all the families, were used to seeing relatives and neighbors leave, and France, Switzerland, Australia, America, Africa were faraway places but at the same time familiar—someone from here, someone from there, they'd all gone to one of these places. In East Africa, they were looking for workers to build roads; the pay wasn't bad, better than France, anyway, probably because of all the discomforts, the wilderness, the life in a barracks with military discipline.

Giacomo didn't want to leave—he had Irene—and he'd become an expert at collecting *recupero*, as good as his father: he knew how to handle bombs, could tell them apart right away, what type, what caliber; he knew how to set them off without blowing them to bits. He could also read the land for signs of war, and when he started digging somewhere, he rarely came up empty. What he found annoying, though, was having to report every Saturday afternoon for pre-military training: having to march in cadres, three abreast, on the wide streets before the Laiten Hills, with that white monument above, alone against the sky.

At night, he'd return home, dead tired, and he'd freshen up at the pump, eat his supper, then go to Irene's, as usual, where they talked about their future together. He had a dream: now that he was old enough, he was waiting for the next chance to sign up to take the forestry militia exam, and then after he served his time, they'd get married. He figured being sent to Piedmont or Friuli or even down south was still better than having to go abroad. So he and Irene would always be together, no getting recalled into service, no marriage by proxy. Not everyone could be as lucky as Matteo, with his beautiful house in Australia.

One November evening, Mario knocked on Giacomo's door. He wanted to let his friend know that the exam announcement he'd been waiting for had been posted. Mario was let into the small, lit kitchen: they'd had electricity these past few months—the first money Giovanni sent from Africa, he'd told them to have it installed. For almost two years now, there'd been a light bulb in the local courtyard, put in by the town, and he'd be damned if his family wasn't going to have electricity, too.

"Evening," Mario said. "I was hoping I could talk to Giacomo. Is he at Irene's?"

"Where else?" Giacomo's grandmother said. "Come on in and wait for him. He should be home soon for supper."

"No, I probably ought to go find him."

"Stay for supper," Giacomo's mother said. "We're having potatoes in bacon fat."

"Thank you, no, Signora Rina. I just have something I need to tell him. Good night. Enjoy your dinner."

He left. It was beginning to snow. On the road from Irene's, he saw Giacomo and told him about the announcement for the forestry militia exam.

"Tomorrow morning, I'm going to the town hall for the forms. I'll get them right away. Thanks, Mario."

"You should probably ask the *GIL* commander to give you a letter saying you were a national *Avanguardista* champion. That might come in handy."

The next morning he went to the forestry service to read the announcement for the exam and to get more information. A sergeant gave him the list of required documents he'd have to present. "A lot of others have been asking, too," the man said. "Competition's going to be stiff."

A deciding factor for being admitted to the exam, though: you had to be a member of a fascist organization, and he hadn't paid his dues in two years, not since he was an *Avanguardista* getting a uniform and skis for competition; then he lost interest and didn't care if he was enrolled or not. And he didn't care about competing anymore. But now what? He gritted his teeth and went to see the commander of the *Giovani Fascisti* at his home.

After saying hello, he told the commander, "It would really help me out if I could have a signed statement saying I'm a member of the *Giovani Fascisti*."

"What for?"

"For the forestry militia exam."

"You, too, huh? But I don't have the records here at the house. Come to fascist headquarters after four o'clock tomorrow. I'll be expecting you."

He left the lieutenant's house and went to the town hall to get the required documents from the Civil Registry Office. He needed stamped papers, revenue stamps, plus he had to pay an administrative fee. The clerk also gave him a sample of how to write out an answer on the four-lire stamped paper. It all cost as much as a good day's *recupero*.

In the afternoon, he went to the local fascist headquarters. The commander took out his register and Giacomo's name was there; he'd been kept in good standing, even though he hadn't paid his dues—the Provincial Federation didn't need to know about those in arrears or those who'd deserted. "I'll write you a letter saying you're enrolled as an active member," the commander said, "and I'll get it signed by the political secretary. Come back in two days. But it looks to me like you haven't paid your dues in two years. In fact, it looks like you've never paid as a *Giovane Fascista*. And why's that?"

"I've been away collecting *recupero* in the Dolomites. I guess I forgot."

"I guess so. And that must be why we never see you at the meetings. Next year, though, you remember to pay. And how about your father? What's he write these days from Africa? You know, anyone enlisting under twenty-one years old needs his parents' permission. Maybe your mother's will be enough. Of course, we should include a note to the *podestà* about your father being in East Africa with our volunteer militia workers."

"Thank you, sir. Thank you so much. I'll come back for the letter."

"In two days, on the Fascist Saturday. We'll see you then."

30

That winter was a long time passing. In early January, the thermometer hovered above zero and one day dropped below it, so that pipes were freezing in many of the houses and districts, and people had to melt snow for water. Mario was supposed to go to Bormio for the national *GIL* ski championships, but he caught the flu and his family wouldn't let him leave with the team. The School of Fascist Culture and the Catholic school organized an evening lecture series on special-interest topics: "Emperor Augustus," "Battle of the Scientists," "The Jesuits from Spain to the Far East," "The Sila Division in East Africa"; university professors came and famous lawyers, military chaplains, monsignors — and the people gladly went to hear them, also because the lecture hall was nice and warm.

The evening of January 25, 1938, was one to remember. It was a cold night, full of stars, but there were also strange clouds to the north, blowing east to west with the high wind. Around eight o'clock, the sky over the northern mountains began turning red, a gloomy red. At first people thought it must be a gigantic forest fire. But in wintertime? With all the snow? And where was the smoke? Little by little, an ever more violent red was filling the sky. The stars disappeared. It was a cold night, close to zero, but the people stood on the streets, eyes fixed on that strange, fascinating, frightening sky. About three hours later, the stars came out again.

The old folks took this as a bad sign, a warning: that red in the sky meant blood, war. The next day the newspapers said it was actually an aurora borealis, an extremely rare phenomenon in our latitudes that probably wouldn't occur again for centuries. But not everyone was convinced: in Spain, the civil war was wreaking endless death and destruction, and this was a sign from Heaven: Mankind, there's still time — stop at once!

Someone else who'd read the Bible insisted this was the second sign of the Apocalypse: in the red clouds on that winter night, he'd seen the red horseman who would "take peace from the land, and people would slit one another's throats, and the horseman would have a great sword." It was just a matter of recognizing that red horseman with the great sword.

As the weeks went by, the war in Spain grew ever more ferocious. One of our fellow townsmen, a famous officer and pilot, was down there with the "Ace of Clubs" Squadron. But we also had anti-fascist emigrants fighting on the Republican side—four died with the International Brigades. This last piece of news reached the Altipiano by way of France, then Schio, the two comrades in *Giovani Fascisti* uniforms riding their bicycles up here to tell us.

In February, a flu epidemic put over half the town in bed. Nino grew very sick: his bronchitis turned to pleurisy, then pneumonia. Doctor Anelli ordered him to stay in bed for a month. One afternoon, Giacomo and Mario went to visit and found Nino looking pale and thin. They couldn't stay long: his mother was worried he'd get too tired. The room reeked of medicine, and a bowl of water with essence of pine oil had been left to evaporate on the fire-brick stove.

When it came time to say goodbye, Giacomo told him, "We'll see you soon. We'll go to Garto's grove in the spring and look for nests"—as if they were still children looking for nests and not young men looking for girls!

In March and April, there was a drought, and the price of hay soared higher than ever; on Saint Mark's Day, April 25, the meadows were covered with snow instead of grass, and the feast of the nearby town, when boys gave girls terra cotta whistles, was pushed back to the first of May. Even then it was sleeting, and some people insisted this, too, was because of the aurora borealis on January 25. But Giacomo's grandmother said there'd always been times of odd weather—folks just had short memories, didn't know how to look to the past. When she was a girl, she'd gone by sled over snowy meadows to the Feast of Saint Mark, and she'd also seen heather and tiny daisies blooming at Christmas.

Like always, in late June and July, the hay was mowed, and at twilight the smell of fermenting hay drifted over the hills, through the streets of town, and into the houses.

On July 17, a Sunday, His Majesty Victor Emanuel III, King of Italy and Albania, Emperor of Ethiopia, came up to inaugurate the *ossario* mounument — "The Sacrarium," the newspapers were calling it. Arches lined the streets; the coats of arms of the Hundred Italian Cities hung from a hundred flag poles; there was a flag in every window. Two regiments of soldiers stood at attention along the Boulevard of Heroes. Airplanes soared over the Sacrarium Roman Arch and dropped flowers and small tri-colored flags. Thousands of veterans had come from all over Italy, and there were generals, bishops, prefects, provincial party secretaries, soldiers, *Giovani Fascisti*, *Avanguardisti*, *Balillas*, *Piccole* and *Giovane Italiane*, representatives from the branches of the military, military bands.

And Giacomo, Mario, and some of their friends lined the way up the stairs for the King-Emperor. When he stepped out of the car, cannon volleys sounded his arrival. Nervously, he climbed the stairs, saber pressed to his side. Right behind him, huffing and puffing, came Count Guglielmo Pecori Giraldi, Italian Field Marshal and Commander of the Altipiano Army. The *carabinieri* band began playing the Royal March.

Three trumpet blasts, and three bishops started celebrating the mass. During moments of silence, the band played "The Song of Piave."

There'd never been so many people up here, so many buses, cars, trucks, bicycles, community bands, military bands, folk groups, banners, flags, pennants. In the meadows groups sat, eating and drinking, and by sunset the streets were filled with drunk people singing war tunes and hymns to the Motherland. At last, with the night, the dead got some peace and quiet. Or were they out that night, too, silent shadows walking the mountains? Maybe Vu would know: he was there with the shepherds.

Marshal Pietro Badoglio sent the following message for that solemn occasion: "In order for the new *Ossario* to be more than merely a shadowy enclosure, all Italians — who have been tested, as have I, in our Imperial conquest — must stay forever worthy of this legacy of faith in the Motherland's great destiny...." And his Excellency, Achille Starace: "The *Ossario* Monument recalls the epic period of our Great War and renews, in the presence of the inviolable Alps, the intrepid, confident roar of Fascist Italy—as led by Il Duce, vindicator of victory and of his forefathers—to the greatness, to the glory of the Empire!"

And Federal Comm. Bruno Mazzaggio: "Fascism and the people of Vicenza shall lift their Emblems and Pennants to the sky and salute the Heroes who gave life and Victory to our Motherland as she climbs to her immortal destiny under our infallible leader, founder of the Empire: IL DUCE."

The illustrious lawyer, Franceschini, Head of the Province, had transcribed the Lord's Prayer, substituting "HEROES" for "Father." Others—generals, Italian academics, poets, and party delegates—did things like this as well.

Two months later, Il Duce came to visit the Veneto. Some strange characters showed up—the town had never seen anything like them. They crept around, peered through windows, over balcony rails, even into drain holes. There were a couple of lumberjack brothers who, whenever they had a few drinks, insisted on being socialist, and there was an emigrant back from the United States who'd dared to say, in the Caffè Nazionale, that a president's better than a king-emperor (if you don't like a president, you can always chuck him); these three were picked up at home by the *carabinieri* and hustled off to the district jail for a few days.

One evening in the piazza, a group of friends, including Mario and Nino, were approached by three shady-looking characters.

"Break it up, you punks!" said one of the men. At first the boys didn't understand, and so the men, hands waving around, repeated this command. Slowly, the friends left; they went to the movies where *Bronze Sentinels* was playing.

Il Duce's day was September 25. The streets leading to the *ossario* monument were cleared, and people crowded along the cordoned roads where "He!—Il Duce!" would be coming. Up by the monument steps stood two war widows, the *podestà* from each of the seven towns of the Altipiano, and a squad of *Giovani Fascisti* to present arms, Giacomo and Mario among them.

Il Duce stepped from the car. He listened, frowning, while the *podestà* of the main town made a speech; he reviewed the squad of *Giovani Fascisti*; he marched into the *ossario*, then right back out after a few minutes. He went up to the terrace to admire the view.

His speech was that afternoon, in Vicenza. Trucks full of fascist youth members and soldiers drove down from the Altipiano to join the thousands of others crammed into the Piazza dei Signori and the nearby streets, everyone listening as Mussolini shouted that Italy was strong, invincible, and that they'd probably soon be at war.

"We're ready now!" the crowd roared: "Du-ce! Du-ce!"

31

Any day now, Giacomo was expecting to hear when he'd go for the exam. Then he learned that others from town had already been called to Rome; he was terribly disappointed, and he went to the forestry department to find out why he'd been excluded. The people there didn't know what to tell him—they didn't understand it themselves. Feeling bitter, Giacomo went back to collecting *recupero*. In late November, just after Mario turned seventeen, he left for Aosta; he'd be attending the central military school of mountaineering called "Duca degli Abruzzi," which offered a training program that specialized in skiing and rock-climbing. In July 1939, Nino was looking for edelweiss and fell from the rocks. His friends held a wake for him in a small chapel after they'd covered him in flowers.

Giacomo went for his military physical; as was the custom, the draftees rang the bells. And that day, too, Giacomo couldn't figure out why the colonel, the president of the draft board, assigned him not to the Alpini forces—like nearly everyone else from town—but to the infantry, so far away. No, he couldn't possibly be aware of the note on the colonel's desk from the criminal records file that included his name and the entry: "Participated in the 1935 strike during construction of the *ossario* monument."

Up in the mountains, with the bright fall weather, Vu was digging away as usual in the trenches. He had about two kilograms of cartridges in his sack and maybe ten kilograms of lead. He was just climbing out of a weapons pit on Cima delle Saette, when he saw a setter-dog in front of him, and then a man. It was Doctor Fabrello, who came up every year on Sundays to hunt mountain pheasants.

"Good afternoon, Albino," the doctor said. "And how are you?"

"Fine, fine. Good day to you. Don't really need a doctor, though.

You pheasant-hunting?"

"Yes, but I'm just looking today—I left my rifle at home. I'll come again after Saint Matthew. So have you seen any?"

"Saw some white pullets on Chiesa. Some pheasants here and there. The shepherds found quite a few this year."

"You hear about the war, Albino?"

"What war?"

"Last Friday, Germany declared war on Poland and yesterday, France and England declared war on Germany."

"Just like before," Vu muttered. "Like in '14." Then he said goodbye and headed for the mule-track, his load of *recupero* over his shoulder.

At the Alpini Spring, he ran into Giacomo: "You heard the news, kid? Doctor Fabrello just told me—the war's started. Get ready."

"War?—what war?"

"The war. Germany against Poland and France and England against Germany. Like in '14. Then it'll be Italy's turn, then Russia's, then America's. Go find your sweetheart. Before you're called up. Don't waste time with *recupero*." And a shadow crossed Vu's face—maybe he was remembering when he'd been drafted that winter of '14, the days full of love before he left, the days full of bitterness when he returned.

"Go home, kid," Vu said now. "I'll look after your *recupero*. I'll make sure they come pick it up from the tunnel, and I'll get you your money. Go. Go find your girl."

Early in the spring of 1940, the *recuperanti* went back to work. By June 10, they were on the slopes of Ortigara, and Nin Sech told them about that same ill-fated day in 1917, when he'd been in the Sette Comuni Battalion, and they'd joined the assault on that mountain. And already—only twenty-three years later—a second world war!

"Just think," Nin said, "I was here once shooting and killing others, and now I'm back looking for bombs to keep myself fed."

They spent the night in a tunnel on Monte Chiesa, not knowing
that late in the long spring afternoon, Mussolini, standing on the

balcony of the Palazzo Venezia, had announced Italy was joining the war alongside Germany. They found this out the following day from Mario Ballot, just back from a tryst in town, who entertained them with his imitation of Il Duce's speech. Sitting having their lunch by the Campigoletti Spring, the men nearly split their sides laughing — except for Nin Sech and Massim, whose faces were hard, grim, their mouths full of polenta suddenly gone bad. Then all at once Nin jumped up, swearing loudly — Nin, who never swore! — and he hurled his pickaxe, grabbed his *recupero* sack, and set off for the Valle dell'Agnella, quietly cursing Fascism and the House of Savoy.

That summer passed quickly; the *recupero* yield was good, and even those who had pre-military duty on Fascist Saturdays never lost a day's work. The districts got their war news off Maria Plebs' radio or by reading soldiers' letters from the front. In the mountains, the *recuperanti* felt free to speak their minds — with no enemy ears around to listen. France fell, and with it the hopes of those in Paris during the Spanish Civil War who'd joined with the Popular Front against Fascism; then came news of the war against Greece. One night at the end of November, a group had gathered at a stable, and someone mentioned what Albino Pûn (now a corporal in the Alpine Artillery) had written home: "Here in Albania, the ground's so hard, we never hoe. We only dig...." And while the censors hadn't caught on, everyone knew hoeing meant advancing and digging meant retreating.

Word also arrived of the first dead in battle: Rocco della Nana, Toni della Casetta Rossa, Bepi Mésele, Bibi. No, this was no longer some boys' game on the slopes of the Laitens or in the trenches on Clema; these men weren't playing dead; and in the houses where they'd received the notices, the doors and windows stayed shut and the archpriest walked about in silence, so he could find those who were crying.

It was about this time that Giacomo received his notice telling him to report for duty. First he took a train to a Piedmont barracks for boot camp. Then he and a group of recruits wandered around by train, back and forth through Italy, in pursuit of a unit he never caught up with because it, too, was always on the move. At last, near Rome, he got his permanent assignment, to the 81st Infantry Regiment of the Turin Division, which, according to General Staff, was part of the motor corps, even if it didn't have any vehicles.

One June day in 1941, Mario, who'd been on special leave following the Greek campaign in Albania, was in Vicenza, waiting to catch the train back to his regiment. He went into the "Troop-Refreshment Room" and there, off in a corner, sitting alone, was Giacomo. Mario walked over, smiling, calling to him. Giacomo got to his feet, at first puzzled by this Alpini sergeant, then astonished, and finally, moved. They hugged each other and both blurted out, "Where are you headed?"

They sat down, silent a moment, and stared at one another. Then Giacomo repeated, "Where are you headed? I have a short pass home. Then I'm leaving for Russia."

"I've been home a month. I was in Albania. Now I'm headed back to my regiment. What's it been, two years, since we saw each other?"

"Time can go by so fast," Giacomo said, "and sometimes so slow. As you can tell, they put me in the infantry. Fate, I guess."

"How's Irene? And your family?"

"Irene's home, waiting for me. It sure would have been better if I'd followed her advice three years back. She thought I ought to go to Australia, to my brother-in-law, Matteo's, and then we could've married by proxy within the year. I waited too long. When I decided to apply for a passport, they told me they couldn't give me one—I had military duty."

"I'm sorry. But this war's bound to be over soon and afterwards, things'll be different. So how's your mother? Your father back from Africa yet?"

"My mother's fine. My father came down with dysentery and returned just before the war broke out. My grandmother died last winter."

"Your grandmother was always so lively, really sharp."

They talked about three men from town who'd died in Albania—one of them, Rocco, had been a classmate of theirs; and they talked about Nino falling from the rocks when he was out picking edelweiss. They remembered ski competitions and girls.

"At home," Giacomo said, "I still have a book you loaned me. I kept it because I liked it."

"What book's that?"

"*Michael Strogoff.* My grandmother read it, too."

"Don't worry about it. When we come back, I'll have some even better ones for you. But can I get you something? Let's have a bite to eat."

They each had a cheese sandwich and a couple of glasses of wine. The train for Milan-Turin was pulling in, and Mario stood up. "Yours should be leaving in about fifteen minutes," he said. "By tonight, you'll be home with Irene and your family. Say hello for me."

Giacomo walked him to the platform. They were quiet now. The train stopped. Mario climbed onto a third-class car; he put his head out the window.

"See you," he said. And then, as if twelve years hadn't gone by, laughing: "Giacomo, can you tell me the classification of the cherry tree?"

Giacomo looked puzzled. Then he laughed, too, and with the train starting to move, he shouted:

"*Dicotyledoneae.* Family *rosaceae.* Genus *prunus.* Species *avium.*"

Six months later, Mario found himself on the Russian front as well. It was the coldest winter of the century, the winter that froze the German war-machine. He'd been assigned, along with other Alpini troops, to teach Italian expeditionary forces to use skis. Only in the military!—waiting until the front to teach soldiers to ski! But when he and the others arrived in Russia, they were assigned instead to the battalion they'd traveled with, the Monte Cervino Ski Battalion, which was made up of a bunch of daredevil volunteers. They'd reached Russia after an endless journey, in the heart of winter. At Yasynuvata, near Stalino, they headed toward Rikovo on foot. One evening they stopped in a village, and Mario and his squad spent the night in an abandoned *izba.* There was still straw on the floor where some soldiers must have slept. And then he noticed something on the smoke-stained wall, words scratched in Italian with a piece of coal:

GREETINGS TO ALL THOSE FROM HOME
WHO PASS THIS WAY

Underneath was Giacomo's full name, his district, and the date, December 18, 1941. Mario smiled, and his heart warmed at the thought of seeing his friend.

32

...In the silent house. A fragment from a 10 mm shell sat on the mantel. I remember why it was there — to hold the tongs for stoking the fire and pulling out the bits of burning wood. Under the bomb fragment, I noticed a slip of paper, folded over. I picked it up, blew off the dust, opened it, and read:

Ministry of War, General Draft Board, Registry Office of Non-Commissioned Officers and Troops: RECORD OF MISSING IN ACTION as pertains to Infantryman _____ compiled by 81st Turin Infantry Regiment Headquarters, dated March 30, 1942: herein is certified by said document that at time of battle taking place December 25, 1941, in Novo Orlowka, Russian Front, infantryman disappeared and subsequent to this date has not been identified among bodies recovered or soldiers captured. In that three months have passed from date of disappearance and all further investigations and inquiries have provided no resultant information regarding said infantryman, it has been deemed impossible to determine whether or not infantryman is still alive or is in fact deceased, and he is therefore reported missing in action as laid down in article 124 of the rules of war as these rules apply.

Note: Present record not valid for purposes of the Registry Office.

GLOSSARY

Alpini: the Italian mountain infantry corps with specialized skills in mountaineering.

Altipiano (also *"altopiano"*): the Asiago Plateau, where the novel takes place, located in the pre-Alps of Vicenza, in the Veneto region; it is also called "L'altopiano dei setti communi," referring to the main town of Asiago and six other communities of this area.

Avanguardista: a fascist youth group for boys, ages 15-18.

Balilla: a fascist youth group for boys, ages 8-14.

Cimbro: the ancient Germanic dialect of the seven communities of the Asiago Plateau. Cimbro has almost completely disappeared from the area.

Donne Fasciste: a fascist group for women.

Giovani Fascisti: boys of the fascist youth group for ages 18-21.

Giovane Italiane: a fascist group for girls.

The Italian Intervention (chapter 8): the passage Giacomo reads aloud refers to the time when the Irredentists advocated Italy's annexing those Italian-speaking areas that Austria still occupied following the Seven Weeks' War (1866).

The Lateran Agreements (chapter 3): Giacomo learns about this agreement whereby Mussolini recognized the Vatican State; the result of the Conciliation of 1929 was that fascist Italy secured the Church's support.

Piccole Italiane: a fascist group for girls.

September 20, 1870 (chapter 3): Giacomo's grandmother refers to this famous day when Italian troops broke through the gates of the Papal State of Rome; the final unification of Italy followed shortly thereafter.

Tönle (chapter 8): this character, mentioned by Giacomo's grandmother, is the protagonist of Mario Rigoni Stern's novel, *Storia di Tönle (The Story of Tönle)*.

National Security Volunteer Militia: the official name for the Italian Blackshirts.

AFTERWORD

Giacomo's Seasons begins and ends with a silent house. This was a real place, a tiny, abandoned home that Mario Rigoni Stern showed me, years ago, when I met him in Asiago to talk about his book. The house stood with a few others on a slope past a grassy airfield. Beyond the house was a long hill, "*il Moor*," leading up to woods. It was summer, and endlessly green.

The stillness of this place was startling and entirely appropriate to this quiet novel, or long story, as Rigoni Stern described it, the third of a trilogy including *La storia di Tönle* (*The Story of Tönle*) and *L'anno della vittoria* ("Victory Year"), which, taken together, speak of the great upheavals of the late nineteenth and early twentieth centuries in Italy, of attempts at nation-building and the devastation of World War I, and of an ancient mountain community in northeastern Italy that is swallowed up in the process.

For an Italian reader, there is much in this historical novel that will seem distant, foreign, as Rigoni Stern lovingly describes the fauna, mountains, and ancient customs of his homeland. Journalist Carlo Sgorlon calls Rigoni Stern a "'sober poet of alpine civilization'" and comments that his writing "'seems distant because the civilization he represents is far removed, silent, sober, discrete.... Rigoni Stern is the poet, reporter, anthropologist, zoologist, animal behaviorist, entomologist, and botanist of this civilization'" (qtd. in Ferguson 161). While the contemporary Italian reader might find many details of the Asiago high plateau to be foreign, the Missing-In-Action notice the narrator discovers in the silent house of his former classmate is something that would resonate. For an American audience, this might not be the case. The notice of the soldier missing, with obvious irony, on December 25, 1941, serves as the quiet precursor of what's in store for the Italians on the Soviet front, almost exactly one year later, when the ill-equipped and ill-trained Italian Eighth Army, sent hastily by Mussolini so as to have some share in the glory alongside Germany, was routed by Soviet forces at Stalingrad. Of the approximately 220,000 soldiers of The Eighth Army deployed on the Don River, little more than half returned to Italy in early 1943. Many were killed in battle; approximately 22,000 men died during the three-hundred mile retreat over the frozen steppe in temperatures of thirty to forty below. 70,000 men were captured by the Red Army; many of these men died on forced marches; on brutal train transports not unlike those headed to German concentration camps; and from starvation and disease in Soviet prisoner-of-war camps. Of these captured soldiers, only 10,000 ever returned to Italy.

In the Eighth Army there were also three divisions, totaling 60,000 men, of Alpini troops specially trained for mountain and winter warfare. While the Don front collapsed, the Alpini Corps held out and would be completely isolated by Soviet forces and would have to break through the Soviet encirclement to rejoin the front. Sergeant Mario Rigoni Stern was among these soldiers. His memoir-novel, *Il sergente nella neve* (Giulio Einaudi Editore, 1953, translated as *The Sergeant in the Snow*, 1954), recounts this experience, and has become an anti-war classic that is widely taught in Italian schools. In a filmed interview, Rigoni Stern states, "The culminating moment of my life wasn't winning literary prizes or writing books; it was when I left the Don in the middle of the night with seventy Alpini and I walked west to get home, and I managed to break out of the stronghold without losing a single man and get away from the front, organizing the retreat — that was my life's masterpiece..." Of those 60,000 Alpini, 35,000 never returned to their mountains.

Ferguson, Ronnie. "The Critique of National Identity in the Novels of Rigoni Stern." *Forum of Modern Language Studies*: 2002 Vol. xxxviii No. 2. 155-169.

Hamilton, Hope. *The Italian Alpine Corps in the Stalingrad Campaign, 1942-1943: Sacrifice on the Steppe* (Haverton and Newbury: Casemate Publishers), 2011.

Mazzacurati, Carlo and Paolini, Marco. *Ritratti: Mario Rigoni Stern*, 1999.